GOLDEN

also

by

# jessi kirby

*Moonglass*

*In Honor*

# GOLDEN

## jessi kirby

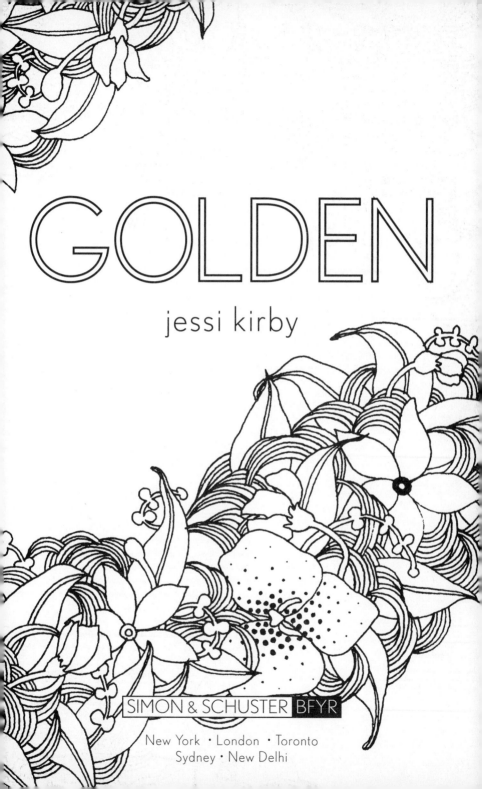

SIMON & SCHUSTER BFYR

New York · London · Toronto
Sydney · New Delhi

An imprint of Simon & Schuster Children's Publishing Division
1230 Avenue of the Americas, New York, New York 10020
Text copyright © 2013 by Jessi Kirby
Illustration copyright © 2013 by Emily Caisip
SIMON & SCHUSTER BFYR
is a trademark of Simon & Schuster, Inc.
For information about special discounts for bulk purchases, please contact
Simon & Schuster Special Sales at 1-866-506-1949
or business@simonandschuster.com.
The Simon & Schuster Speakers Bureau can bring authors to your live event.
For more information or to book an event, contact the Simon & Schuster Speakers Bureau
at 1-866-248-3049 or visit our website at www.simonspeakers.com.
Book design by Lizzy Bromley
The text for this book is set in Weiss.
Manufactured in the United States of America
2 4 6 8 10 9 7 5 3 1
Library of Congress Cataloging-in-Publication Data
Kirby, Jessi.
Golden / Jessi Kirby. — 1st ed.
p. cm.
Summary: "Seventeen-year-old Parker Frost has never taken the
road less traveled. Valedictorian and quintessential good girl, she's about to
graduate high school without ever having kissed her crush or broken the rules.
So when fate drops a clue in her lap—one that might be the key to unraveling a
town mystery—she decides to take a chance."—Provided by publisher.
ISBN 978-1-4424-5216-9 (hardback) — ISBN 978-1-4424-5225-1 (eBook)
[1. Choice—Fiction. 2. Conduct of life—Fiction. 3. Mothers and daughters—Fiction.
4. Diaries—Fiction. 5. Love—Fiction. 6. Family problems—Fiction.] I. Title.
PZ7.K633522Gol 2013
[Fic]—dc23
2012042216

FIRST
EDITION

For my grandma,

MARIETTA,

who introduced me

to the simple beauty

of Frost's words,

and my grandpa,

GERARD,

who always

believed

in mine

# life is made of moments. and choices.

Not all of them matter, or have any lasting impact. Skipping class in favor of a taste of freedom, picking a prom dress because of the way it transforms you into a princess in the mirror. Even the nights you steal away from an open window, tiptoe silent to the end of the driveway, where darkened headlights and the pull of something unknown beckon. These are all small choices, really. Insignificant as soon as they're made. Innocent.

But then.

Then there's a different kind of moment. One when things are irrevocably changed by a choice we make. A moment we will play endlessly in our minds on lonely nights and empty days. One we'll search repeatedly for some indication that what we chose was right, some small sign that tells us the truth isn't nearly as awful as it feels. Or as awful as anyone would think if they knew.

So we explain it to ourselves, justify it enough to sleep. And then we bury it deep, so deep we can almost pretend it never happened. But as much as we wish it were different, the truth is, our worlds are sometimes balanced on choices we make and the secrets we keep.

## 1.

"To a Thinker"
*—1936*

There's no such thing as a secret in this town. But I'm keeping this one, just for today. I fold the letter once, twice, three times and slide it into my back pocket like a golden ticket, because that's what it is. A ticket out. Being chosen as a finalist for the Cruz-Farnetti Scholarship is my version of winning the lottery. It means Stanford pre-med and everything else I've worked for.

Icy wind sears my cheeks red as I cross the school parking lot, and I curse Johnny Mountain for being right when he forecast the late spring storm. If the biting wind and swirling white sky are any indication, we may be graduating in the snow, which is not at all how I pictured it. But today I don't *really* mind. Today the wind and I burst through the double doors together, and it carries me like someone who's going places, because now it's official. I am.

Kat's already at my locker when I get there and it gives me the smallest pause. We don't keep secrets from each other. Her eyes run over me, top to bottom, and she smiles slowly. "*You* look like you're in a good mood." It's more friendly accusation than casual greeting, and she punctuates it by leaning back against the blue metal of the lockers and waiting expectantly.

"What? I can't be in a good mood?" I reach around her and spin the lock without looking at the numbers, try to hide my smile.

She shrugs and steps aside. "*I'm* not. This weather sucks. Mountain says it's gonna be the worst storm in ten years or some bullshit like that. I'm *so* over the frickin' snow. It's May. We should be wearing tiny shorts and tank tops instead of . . . this." She looks down at her outfit in disdain.

"Well," I say, trying to pull my mind away from visions of the red-tiled roofs and snowless breezeways of Stanford, "you look cute anyway."

Kat rolls her eyes, but straightens up her shoulders the slightest bit and I know that's exactly what she wanted to hear. She stands there looking effortless in her skinny jeans, tall boots, and a top that falls perfectly off one shoulder, revealing a lacy black bra strap. Really, cute isn't the right word for her. The last time she was cute was probably elementary school. By the time we hit seventh grade, she was hot and all its variations, for a couple more reasons than just her tumbling auburn hair. That was the year Trevor Collins nicknamed the two of us "fire and ice," and it stuck. In the beginning I thought the whole "ice" thing had something to do with my last name (Frost), or maybe my eyes (blue), but over the years, it's become increasingly clear that's not what he meant. At all.

Kat shuts my locker with a flick of her wrist as soon as I unlock it. "So. There's a sub for Peters today, a cute one I'd normally stick around for, but I'm starving and Lane's working at Kismet. Let's get outta here and eat. He'll give us free drinks and I'll have you back by second period. Promise." She's about to come up with another inarguable reason for me to ditch with her when Trevor Collins strolls up. Even after this long, that's still how I think of him. Trevor Collins. It was how he introduced himself when he walked into Lakes High in seventh grade with a winning smile, natural charm, and the confidence to match.

His eyes flick to me, not Kat, and heat blooms in my cheeks. "Hey, Frost. You look saucy today. Feelin' adventurous?" He dangles a lanyard in front of me, and a smile hovers at the corners of his mouth. "I got the keys to the art supply closet, and *I* could have you back before first period even starts. Promise." He hits me with a smile that lets me know he's joking, but I wonder for a second what would happen if I actually said yes one of these days.

I meet his eyes, barely, before opening my locker so the door creates a little wall between us, then give my best imitation of disinterested sarcasm. "Tempting." But between his dyed black hair and crystal blue eyes, it kind of is. I have no doubt a trip to the art supply closet with him would be an experience. Half the female population at Lakes High would probably attest to it, which is exactly why it'll never happen. I like to think of it as principle. And standards. Besides, this has been our routine since we were freshmen, and I like it this way, with possibility still dancing between us. From what I've seen, it's almost always better than reality.

Kat blows him a kiss meant to send him on his way. "She can't. We're going to get coffee. And she's too good for you. And you have a girlfriend, jackass." There's that, too, I remind myself. But I've never really counted Trevor's girlfriends as legitimate, seeing as they don't generally last beyond being given the title.

"Actually, I'm not," I say a little too abruptly. "Going to get coffee, I mean." I shut my locker and Trevor raises an eyebrow, jingling his keys. "I uh . . . I can't skip Kinney's today. He's got some big project for me." Oh, the lameness.

Kat rolls her eyes emphatically. "You don't *actually* have to show up to class when you're the TA and it's last quarter. You do realize that, right?"

"*You* don't have to," I say, matching her smart-ass tone, "because Chang has no idea she even has a TA. Kinney actually realizes I'm supposed to be there."

The bell rings and Trevor takes a step backward, holding up the keys again. "Best four minutes you ever had, Frost. Going once, twice . . ."

I wave him off with a grin, then turn back to Kat, who's now giving me her *you know you want to* look. "Never," I say. I know what's coming next, and I'm hoping that's enough to squash it.

But it's not, because as we walk, she bumps my hip with hers. "C'mon, P. You know you want to. *He's* wanted to since forever."

"Only because *I* haven't."

"Maybe," she shrugs. "But still. School's gonna end, you're gonna wish that just once, you'd done something I would do."

I stop at Mr. Kinney's doorway. Now it's me with the smile. "You mean *did*, right? Because I distinctly remember my best friend being the first girl here to kiss Trevor Collins."

"That was in seventh grade. That doesn't even count." A slow smile spreads over her lips. "Although for a seventh grader, he was a pretty good kisser."

I just look at her.

*"Fine,"* Kat says in her dramatic Kat way that communicates her ongoing disappointment every time I plant my feet firmly on the straight and narrow road. "Go to class. Spend the last few weeks of your senior year pining over the guy you could have in a second while you're at it. I'll see you later." She smacks me on the butt as she leaves, right where my letter is, and for a second I feel guilty about not telling her because this letter means that Stanford has gone from far-off possibility to probable reality. But leaving Kat is also a reality at this point, and I don't think either one of us is ready to think about that yet.

When I step through Kinney's door, future all folded up in my back pocket, he's headed straight for me with an ancient-looking box. "Parker! Good. I'm glad you're here. Take these." He practically throws the box into my arms.

"Senior class journals, like I told you about. It's time to send them out." His eyes twinkle the tiniest bit when he says it, and that's the reason kids love him. He keeps his promises.

I nod, because that's all I have time to do before he goes on. Kinney drinks a lot of coffee. "I want you to go through them like we talked about. Double-check the addresses against the directory, which'll probably take you all week, then get whatever extra postage they need so I can send them out by the end of the month, okay?" He's a little out of breath by the time he finishes, but that's how he always is, because he's high-strung in the best kind of way. The million miles a minute, jump up on the table in the middle of teaching to make a point kind of way.

Before I can ask any questions, he's stepped past me to hold the door open for the sleepy freshmen filing in. Most of them look less than excited for first period, but Mr. Kinney stands there with his wide smile, looks each one of them in the eye, and says "Good morning," and even the grouchy-looking boys with their hoods pulled up say it back.

"Mr. Kinney?" I lug the box of journals a few steps so I'm out of their way. "Would you mind if I take these to the library to work on them?"

"Not at all." He winks and ushers me on my way with the swoop of an arm. "See you at the end of the period." Right on cue, the final bell rings and he swings his classroom door shut without another word.

I linger a moment in the emptied hallway and peek through the skinny window in his door as students get out their notebooks to answer the daily writing prompt they've become accustomed to by this point in the year. Sometimes it's a question, sometimes a quote or artwork he throws out there for them to explain. Today it's a poem, one I'm deeply familiar with, since my dad has always claimed we're somehow, *possibly*, long-lost, distant relatives of the poet himself.

I read the eight lines slowly, even though I know them by heart. Today though, they hang differently in my mind—too heavily. Maybe it's the unwelcome, swirling wind outside, or the fact that so much in my life is about to change, but as I read them, I feel like I have to remind myself that just because someone wrote them doesn't make them true. I would never want to believe they were true. Because according to Robert Frost, "nothing gold can stay."

## 2.

"A breeze discovered my open book
And began to flutter the leaves to look"
—*"A CLOUD SHADOW," 1942*

The tape sealing the box of journals snaps like a firecracker when I jab my pen into it. Ms. Moore, the librarian, looks up from her computer momentarily then goes back to scanning in books in a quick rhythm of beeps just like at the grocery store. I've come here plenty of times before to do projects for Mr. Kinney, so she doesn't question me. I settle in, happy with the small measure of freedom, but when I look down at the open box packed tight with sealed manila envelopes and realize what a pain it's going to be to track down every single address, I half wish I would've taken Kat up on her offer to ditch.

The other half of me wishes I had Mr. Kinney for English this year and not just my TA period. So I could be a part of this. Every year he makes a big show of gifting each of his seniors one of those black-and-white marbled composition books after spring break. Their only assignment for the remainder of the school year is to write in it. Fill it up with words that make a picture of who they are, things they may forget later on, after so many years, and want to look back on. Sort of a letter to their future selves. I know this because Kat did get Kinney, and the day she got her journal she started writing in it like crazy, which is funny since she doesn't usually care about assignments she's going to get a grade on, let alone work that won't count for anything.

But that's where Mr. Kinney's a genius. He realizes that all of us are a little self-absorbed. It's human nature. And so when his students get a chance to preserve what they see as important and worthy about themselves, they do. Then on graduation day, they hand over their journals, all sealed up with hope and pride and secrecy. And ten Junes later, those same kids who are now legitimate grownups get a brief little chapter of their teenage lives in the mail.

I know if I asked he'd give me a journal and let me slip it in with the others so that in a decade I could read the words of my seventeen-year-old self. More than once I've thought about it. But every time I do I come back to the same thought—what if ten years from now I got a chance to read about who I'd been, and I regretted it. What if I read it and saw past the accomplishments, straight through to all the things I missed while I was busy chasing them. I might wish I had done things differently.

The envelopes in the box are lined up neatly and sealed with a clear strip of undisturbed tape across each flap. Mr. Kinney's done this project for so long that even if he did get curious and peek in the beginning, the musings of high school seniors probably didn't hold his attention for very long.

I grab my first stack, bring them over to the computer station and put in Kinney's password. Once I'm in the alumni directory, the first few go quickly since they're in alphabetical order and they're post office boxes that haven't changed, according to the computer. It's not all that surprising, since a lot of people don't ever really leave town. I vaguely recognize one or two of the names, but wouldn't be able to put a face to them. It's small here, but not small enough that you actually know *everyone*. On the other hand it can feel like everyone you run into somehow knows *you*. Or your mom, in my case.

I roll through the first few names, and pretty soon I've got a rhythm and a system, and I can check addresses and daydream at the same time. Only now Stanford may not qualify as a daydream. It feels infinitely more real since yesterday, when I found the thin envelope from the Cruz Foundation in my mailbox. Much different from the early acceptance letter that came months ago. The excitement and relief that letter brought were all tempered with the knowledge that there are hundreds of thousands of dollars between getting in and actually being able to go. It was why I'd spent every waking moment of my life since then searching for ways to make it happen.

And now I have one in my back pocket. So today, instead of running numbers through my head, or wondering if I should've revised the application essays one more time, I let myself replay the morning exchange with Trevor. And I revise that instead. In this new version, when he dangles the keys in front of me, *I'm* the one who raises an eyebrow, right before I take them from his hand and lead him, dumbfounded, to the art closet.

I've never actually been in there, but in my mind's eye, it's dimly lit, with tubes of paint and coffee cans full of brushes lining the shelves—things that might go clattering to the floor if I were brave enough to ever meet his eyes longer than a second. And since it's my daydream, I am, and I do. Trevor smiles in slow motion as he tilts his chin down to kiss me after six years' worth of missed chances, and then—

The name on the next envelope snaps me back like a rubber band. I stare. Breathe. Stare some more.

*Julianna Farnetti.*

I look around, chilled. That can't be right. But it's right there in front of me, written in black ink with big loopy pen strokes just as gorgeous as she was. My first impulse is to see if anyone else saw. The clock ticks away the seconds on the wall. In one row of stacks are a couple of younger girls whispering and trying to look like they're looking for books to check out. Ms. Moore's keeping tabs on them from behind her computer, and the library TA, a tragically nerdy boy named Jake, shoves a book back onto the shelf then straightens out the ones around it for the millionth time. None of them look at me, but I'm nervous all of a sudden because right now it feels like I'm holding in my hands something I shouldn't be. Like I've just brushed my fingers over a ghost. And by all accounts and definitions, I have.

Every town has its stories. Stories that have been told so many times by so many different people they've worked themselves into the collective consciousness as truth. Julianna Farnetti is one of Summit Lakes'. Shane Cruz is the other. And theirs—it's a story of perfection lost on an icy road. They were one of those golden couples, the kind everyone adores and envies at the same time. Meant to be together forever. Teenage dream realized.

And both of them are frozen in time on a billboard at the edge of town for everyone to see. From behind a thick layer of plexiglass that's replaced every few years, they smile their senior portrait smiles like they don't know people have stopped looking for them. Somewhere along the line, the words on the billboard changed from MISSING to IN LOVING MEMORY OF, and I can remember thinking how sad that was, but it was bound to happen. Their parents buried empty coffins.

And still, we have the plaque in the gym, with a picture of Shane and Julianna together, his graduation gown arms wrapped tight around her shoulders and her cap crooked on top of her curly blond hair, both of them laughing like life was about to begin. His family started the scholarship in their name. Hers left town. And still, after ten years, they smile those frozen smiles that never age. Trapped behind the glass and the stories we've come up with for what happened to them.

I glance down again, read the name to be sure. Here in

my hand is Julianna Farnetti's senior journal. Pages she wrote before all of that, when the world was still at her perfect fingertips. When Mr. Kinney told her to capture herself in words she could read later.

There's a post office box on the envelope, but it's worthless. None of her family lives here anymore, and I don't blame them. For a long time after, people talked. Speculated. Investigated. Eventually, the case closed and she and Shane became another town story that weaves its way back to the surface on stormy winter nights. And of course, before graduation. That's when the *Summit Times* runs a tribute to the two of them in the same edition that features the current graduating class. That's also when the old-timer search-and-rescue guys remember over coffee the fierceness of the storm the night they disappeared. The ones who found Shane's mangled Jeep at the bottom of the gorge, half-submerged in the icy river, will talk about how their feet were instantly frostbitten as they plunged in for the two teens who were most surely trapped in the car. At this they shake their heads, maybe mutter "Such a shame," and go back to their regular business, not wanting to linger in the memory of it too long.

I breathe slowly, turn the envelope over in my hands, check the flap that's still sealed up tight. How did nobody think to ask about this? How did Mr. Kinney not open it? Not even out of curiosity about this girl-turned-myth? Maybe he didn't even realize it was there with the others. Or maybe he did, but left it alone out of respect once the official statement came out that they were swept down the river and into Summit Lake, where the search had to end because of the piercing cold and plunging depth of the water. It'd be too sad after that. Like reading *Romeo and Juliet* and knowing all along how it's going to end.

I flip the envelope back over to the side with her name and run my finger over it, teetering on the edge of something. The thing I should do, the most right thing to do, would be to give it to Mr. Kinney and let him decide how to handle it. I don't let myself even think about actually reading it; that would be wrong for so many reasons.

Except.

It feels like history in a manila envelope. Like something that should be saved. My heart beats a touch quicker.

Kat would take it in a second if she were here. She wouldn't even wait to open it. If she were here, I'd be the one to insist we put it back, because that's what I do. It's the role I play between the two of us—conscience to her temptations, reason to her impulsiveness. It's also the role she's always trying to get me to step out of, just a little. She never stops talking about the idea of pivotal moments in life, tiny ones that can either pass you by or make some big dramatic change somewhere down the line, depending on what you choose to do with them. This feels like one of those moments.

I know it's wrong to take it, I do. But something in me decides to do it anyway, and it's so quick and resolute I don't have time to change my mind. I know the period's almost over so I put Julianna's journal on the bottom of the stack and walk it back over to the table where the box and my backpack sit undisturbed. I smile politely at Ms. Moore when she looks up, and when she goes back to her work, I take a deep breath and slide the bottom envelope into my backpack, zip it up quick. The bell rings, sealing my decision, and I have to hurry to get the rest of the journals in the box so I can get it back to Mr. Kinney like it's any normal day and any normal project he's given me to do. But as I step into the hall with the box in my hands and the stolen journal in my bag, I feel like I'm setting foot down a new road. One I've never traveled.

### 3.

"But bid life seize the present?
It lives less in the present
Than in the future always,
And less in both together
Than in the past."

*—"CARPE DIEM," 1938*

I pull out a red chair with a swirly sun painted on it and sit down with my chai. Try to sound casual. "Do you know where Julianna Farnetti's family moved away to?"

Kat gives me a weird look from across the table and leans over her steaming cup. "That's random. No." She takes a sip of her mocha and licks the whipped cream off her lips in a way only she can, which makes her new favorite coffeehouse worker smile as he puts his head down and pretends to wipe the table next to us. Since Lane started working a month ago, Kat's become quite the coffee drinker, if you count white mochas and caramel frappucinos, which I don't, really. He's cute in the way most ski bum seasonal employees are—tan face from days spent on the mountain, scruffy, I-don't-care hair, easygoing smile. Not hard to pull off when you work just enough to pay for a winter of snowboarding and the weed to go with it.

He's doing a really great job on that table, but doesn't say anything, so she doesn't either. Instead, she pretends to focus on our conversation. "Where did that come from, anyway?" As she asks, her eyes slide past me to follow him across the café to the counter.

"I don't know," I shrug. "I was just wondering." I haven't decided yet if I'm going to tell Kat what's in my backpack in the front seat of her car. She'd have to read it as soon as she knew, and I haven't even made up my mind that *I'm* going to read it yet. "Something made me think of her and I just . . . wondered where they went." It's not a total lie. I did, at one point in the day, decide the right thing to do would be to track down her parents and send the intact envelope to them. But then the thought seemed almost cruel.

Kat finally brings her eyes back to me. "I don't think anybody knows where they went. It's not like they had a whole lot of reason to keep in touch after. They just left and never looked back." She takes another slow sip of her coffee and leans back in her chair. "You know, just like you will when you go off to college and leave me here to become a bad, small-town cliché."

She winks at me and I kick her under the table. "*Shut* up." I know she's mostly joking, and I try to sound like I am too, but at the moment, the letter in my back pocket feels like a weight around my neck. I need to just tell her and get it over with. "I told you, you should come with me," I say instead. "You could get a job and we could have a cute little apartment near whatever school I go to, and we can share clothes and order takeout and live happily ever after."

It doesn't come out sounding as plausible as I want it to since I know it's not. Kat will end up staying here because the mess that is her mom will make her feel like she has to. Where my mom drives me insane with her never-ending sermons on how important it is that I achieve more and do better than she did, Kat's seems to wonder why her daughter should ever want or deserve anything beyond a job that barely pays the bills, an endless string of guys she hopes will, and the resulting need to find comfort in a bottle when they don't. Kat's been privy to her mom's drama all her life and mostly brushes it off, but it sometimes makes me sad for her.

"Come on," I say. "Come with me."

She rolls her green eyes, then levels them right at me. "I'm not gonna tag along to college with you. Really. How could I leave *this*?" She sweeps her arm at the wide window in the front of the shop. In the pale afternoon light, the weather-worn buildings across the street sag beneath the last of the snow in a way that complements her sarcasm just right, and I feel like a horrible person for not telling her first thing this morning. I clear my throat.

"I'm a finalist. For the Cruz-Farnetti Scholarship." I say it more to my chai than to Kat.

She leans back and practically yells to the whole place. "Did you just tell me that my best friend is up for the no-joke, tenth anniversary, *full* ride scholarship to frickin' *Stanford?*" I nod again, and in less than a second she's out of her chair, with her arms wrapped around me in a hug that's solid and proud and the slightest bit uncomfortable since my face is smooshed into her boobs. "Holy. *Shit*, Parker!" A lady in the corner shoots us a glare that doesn't bother Kat in the least. "When did you find out?" She pulls back so I can answer, ready to hear all the details, and I'm relieved because she looks happy for me. Genuinely happy.

"The letter came yesterday. I haven't even told my mom yet because I know as soon as I do she'll be on my back about writing the perfect speech. That's the biggest part of their selection process, and it's gonna be the hardest. I basically have to get up and somehow convince the entire board that I'm the one they should give hundreds of thousands of dollars to."

Kat waves a dismissive hand. "Please. You've aced every essay you've ever written, mine included. You're gonna get it."

I laugh, but apprehension seeps into my stomach. "I don't even have any ideas on how to start."

"You will," she says, with a certainty that makes me feel a little better. "You'll figure it out and come up with something brilliant, and then you can put all your energy into more important things. Like Trevor Collins." She sits back in her chair and smiles, shakes her head. "I *knew* there was something you were sitting on. You're a shitty secret keeper."

"I wasn't keeping it secret, I was just . . . waiting for the right time to tell you 'cause I didn't know . . ." I don't want to say I didn't know how she'd take it once it became a real thing that might actually happen.

She lets me fumble a moment before reaching across the table for both my hands. "P, all that crap I give you about leaving is just that—crap. I'm happy for you, I really am. I'm gonna miss you like crazy, but this is *huge*. And well-deserved. We should celebrate."

Before I can answer, the bell above the door jingles and Josh, the owner of the place, strides in, the smell of cold swirling all around him. He nods at us. "Ladies."

"Hi," I say, and look down at the table, wondering what I could possibly add to that. Josh intimidates me. He's older than us by more than a few years, with perfectly messy dark hair, warm brown eyes, and tattoos up and down his arms—which I normally wouldn't find attractive, but they're intriguing on him. He's good-looking in a quiet, unassuming way that somehow reduces me to one word answers and makes me wonder what he's really like. Kat and I have been in a lot over the years, but he's never said anything to us that wasn't necessary for business. Not that he's rude or anything. He just seems like one of those people who'd rather keep to themselves.

"Mocha's perfect today," Kat chimes in.

"Good to hear," he says. He gives her one more little smile, not the flirty one she's looking for, but one that says he's just being polite, then heads back to the counter that

Lane is making sure is spotless. I watch a moment as Josh sets his package down and fills a tall cup of coffee, greets Lane with a pat on the back, then surveys his café/gallery. It's a small, cozy space covered in art that is always changing. Paintings of all different sizes and styles cover every inch of available wall space, and above us, metal mobiles sway gently, their pieces clinking softly together before settling back into place. I've always assumed that somewhere on the walls Josh has a piece or two of his own hanging up, just because he has that whole ex-art student look, but I've never asked.

"I think he's depressed," Kat whispers to me, watching Josh out of the corner of her eye.

"Because he didn't flirt back when you batted your eyelashes and leaned on your boobs just now?"

"No," she says. "Because he doesn't act interested in anyone. Ever. He just walks around with his head down all the time, which is a shame since he's so goddamn good-looking."

"He's also way too old for us."

"I don't know," Kat says, with a wicked grin. "I bet he's not even thirty yet."

"Okay then. Maybe he's just smart enough not to have any interest in seventeen-year-olds."

She sighs. "There is so much you don't understand about guys, P." We both watch him move around behind the counter, seemingly oblivious to the fact that he's our topic of conversation. And that we're staring.

Kat shrugs. "Maybe he's gay."

"He's not gay," I say. "And you're whispering too loud."

"Whatever." Kat shakes her head, but the grin creeps back across her face. "So. How are we gonna celebrate your shiny scholarship letter? Dinner? Hot tubs? Trevor Collins?"

"Oh my God, *stop* already. We can't celebrate yet. Not until I actually win it." I take the last sip of my chai and slide my chair back. "I should probably stop by the store and tell my mom. Maybe she'll be so happy she'll let me go out or something crazy like that."

Kat lays a dramatic hand on her chest. "On a *school* night?"

"There's a first for everything," I say. "You wanna give me a ride?"

She waits a beat before answering, eyeing me carefully. "Only if you promise me one thing."

"What?" I'm sure it's going to be something about not forgetting her or keeping in touch when I leave, and of course that goes without saying.

She leans in and grabs both of my hands again. "Now that you're going, and it's all official, promise me that for the rest of the year you'll ease up and actually enjoy the little bit of high school that's left."

"What are you talking about?" I try to pass it off lightly, like I don't know, but I do. Kat's whole philosophy on life can be summed up in two words: carpe diem (which it is, in loopy script, tattooed on her wrist). Seize the day, live in the moment, soak it all up—good or bad. Which is fine for her. I just happen to think more long term, I guess.

"You know what I mean. High school's almost over, Parker, and what do you have to show for it?"

"Seriously?"

"I mean *besides* your GPA, and Stanford, and valedictorian and all that crap—which I'm totally proud of you for. I'm not knocking those things. But when's the last time you took a chance? Or didn't do what someone else expected of you? Or did something you really wanted to, even though you probably shouldn't have?"

I run my finger around the rim of my empty mug, think about Julianna Farnetti's journal tucked in my bag with the rest of my books, and I lie. "I don't know . . ."

She smacks a hand on the table, sending a splash of mocha from her cup. "Well, it's time. It's time to do something worth remembering."

"Like what?" I ask, humoring her. "What wild and crazy things should I be out doing?"

Kat shakes her head. "You're missing the point. You don't need to go out and do anything wild or crazy. Just do something unexpected for once." She sits back in her chair and looks at me like it's the simplest thing in the world. "Just one thing."

Again, I picture the manila envelope with Julianna Farnetti's writing on it, stuffed between the books in my bag. I open my mouth, and I almost tell her I might have already done a thing like that, and that I don't even know why. Instead, I match the friendly challenge of her tone. "Okay. One thing."

"*Good.*" She drains the remaining mocha from her cup and grabs her purse. "You better make it a worthwhile thing, though. Something big."

"Unexpected, worthwhile, and big," I say. "I'll get right on that."

We both stand, and she loops her arm through mine, face all business. "Okay. Let's go then. Who knows what's out there waiting for you."

# 4.

"I never dared be radical when young
For fear it would make me conservative when old."
— *"PRECAUTION," FROM "TEN MILLS," 1936*

"You were meant for this, Parker." My mom beams. "This. Right here." She holds the creased letter in front of her like it's something holy. Then she frowns. "I just wish you would've kept it nice so we could frame it."

I make a conscious effort not to roll my eyes. "It's just a piece of paper, Mom. And it's not a sure thing. I still have to write the speech—and, you know, win, so don't get all excited yet." I sound like a brat, even to myself, but I can't help it. Now that it's in her hands, I wish I'd kept it to myself just a little longer, because all of a sudden it seems more her accomplishment than mine. And because I know our world will now revolve around me writing and practicing my speech. I snap my chopsticks apart and rub them together hard without saying anything else.

"I'm just so proud of you, honey. I *know* how hard you've worked, and that I haven't always been easy on you, but . . . it's all come down to this. They'll choose you, I just know it." She purses her lips together and her eyes flood behind her glasses. "I always knew you had the potential."

I cringe inwardly, but force a smile. "I know, Mom." Then I raise my steaming bowl of miso so she can continue if she wants to. In the last few years I've learned it's easiest this way. She talks, I mostly listen, sometimes nod, and let her say what she needs to. Especially when it's about "potential," which, in her eyes, is the worst possible thing I could waste. I'm positive it's all tied to my dad and the fact that after publishing his first collection of poetry years ago, he's yet to finish anything else—if you exclude their marriage. I have a feeling that was over before it really began though. My parents are far too different for me to believe they were ever meant to be.

"Have you told your father yet?" she asks in the false casual tone reserved for talking about him.

"Not yet." Her face lights up a bit, and I know it makes her happy that she's the first of them to know, which just seems petty to me, but that's what it's come to.

"Well. You should call him tonight with your good news. Maybe it'll inspire him somehow to know that *you've* accomplished what you set out to do."

She speaks the words lightly, but they're laced together

with sarcasm. It doesn't seem to matter to her that he's now teaching writing at a school in New York, which most people would consider a successful endeavor. But not her. At any mention of it, she's more than happy to discuss her opinion that he's hiding behind helping other people with their writing because he can't do it himself anymore. I change the subject. "Can I go out with Kat for a little while tonight, to celebrate?"

She shakes her head—a reflex she can't help when Kat is involved. "Let's not get ahead of ourselves. You still have a speech to write. Besides, isn't that what we're doing right now? Celebrating?" She gestures at the spread of sushi in front of us.

"Yeah . . . but she wants to take me out for coffee or dessert or something. Just for a little while?" I watch her perfectly made-up face for a sign of compromise, but get only the inflexibility I expect.

"It's a school night, Parker. And you already had coffee."

"What?"

"Debbie Monroe said you and Kat were at Kismet today, and that she wasn't exactly being polite." She stabs a piece of salmon with her chopsticks. "You know, that girl really needs to be more aware of how she acts in public."

I literally have to bite my tongue to keep from answering back the way I really want to. Kat has been "that girl" to my mother for as long as we've been friends, and the way she says it never fails to remind me just what she thinks of her.

"Mom, Debbie Monroe thinks everyone under the age of twenty is either on drugs or involved in some other 'illicit

teenage activities.' She actually said that. In line at the grocery store, and she wasn't joking." I stir up the cloud of miso
that's settled in the bottom of my bowl. "She doesn't know
what she's talking about. Kat wasn't doing anything wrong;
she was just excited for me."

My mother doesn't say anything. Just pinches another
slice of salmon roll between her chopsticks and adjusts her
glasses, and there's my answer.

"Fine," I say into my soup. It's useless to argue. Even more
useless to think that she could bend, just a little, or trust me
for once. I've never given her reason not to—but then again,
I've never had the opportunity either.

My mother lets out a heavy sigh. "Parker, *soon*. Soon
enough you'll be making your own choices. Humor me in
the meantime, okay?"

I look at her, hair pulled back sleek and tight, smile to
match, and decide to see if I can finish my celebratory dinner
without saying anything else. It's surprisingly easy. While
she goes on about the rigors (and cost) of Stanford, all of
which I'm well aware of, thank you, I think about what Kat
said and try to decide what worthwhile, unexpected thing I
could do. I would love, more than anything, to have the guts
to stand up right here and tell my mom to just lay off it all—
the expectations, the pressure, the constant judging—all of
it. A tiny part of me would love to just tell her to forget it.
To say never mind, I don't want any of it. But that's not what
Kat meant.

She meant I should do something unexpected that would
leave me with something I could keep and remember. An

experience instead of a goal. And I get what she means. She's right about me not having very many of those to show for four years of high school. But it seems to me that the experiences that stay with you, the things you'll always remember, aren't the ones you can force, or go looking for. I've always thought of those things as the ones that somehow find you.

5.

"Love and a Question"
—*1913*

By the time we get home my mom has outlined how she thinks my entire speech should go, including all the keywords I should include to ensure that I'm the foundation's obvious choice. I'm actually thankful because as soon as we walk through the door, it gives me the perfect excuse to head upstairs and "get started right away."

"That's my girl," she says, smiling at my unfailing dedication. "Strike while the iron is hot and the inspiration is fresh."

I stop at the top of the stairs and do my best to smile back. Then I walk into my room and close the door behind me. I need a moment. A moment to breathe, because the combination of expectation and good intentions feels especially suffocating tonight. In the quiet of my room, I drop my bag to the floor, flop onto the bed, and exhale. Finally.

Like a reflex my eyes travel up to the ceiling above me, where in ninth grade, in a small act of rebellion, I pinned a poster I'd made for English. My final project for *Romeo and Juliet*. My mom had just had the house painted after my dad moved out, and she decreed there would be no more pin holes in my walls. But she didn't say anything about the ceiling, so I put it up—a collage of images: the sun and moon and stars, a rose, a balcony, a kiss in silhouette, and a tiny glass vial, all under the glittery caption, IT WAS WRITTEN IN THE STARS. It wasn't a masterpiece by any means, and I didn't even get the top score, but it meant something to me. I was in love with the idea of it all—the stars, and fate, and these two people who loved each other enough to want to die without the other. My parents didn't love each other enough to even make eye contact anymore.

It took my mom awhile to notice what I'd done, and she was angry when she did, but too distracted to follow through on making me take it down. Divorce will do that. I don't think she even realizes it's there anymore. It's easy to forget to look up when all you do is focus on the road straight ahead. Which is what I *should* be doing right now. Actually getting started on my speech. But the thought of sitting down to a blank page is so daunting, I don't move. I lie there instead, looking up at love idealized and wondering what it would be like to feel that way. And then, all in one motion, I do move. Up and across the room to where my bag leans against the wall.

I take the stolen envelope out slowly, feeling every ounce of its weight in my hands, and then I bring it to my desk, sit down, and stare at it until Julianna's name goes blurry. For half a second I let myself think that maybe it's not coincidence I found it today. Maybe it found me, for whatever reason. Then I almost laugh at how ridiculous that sounds. I'm reaching. Justifying the thing I want to do.

I get up. Pace. Slide my window open. The wind has died down outside, but the air that drifts in still has a bite to it that hints at snow. It's too cold to climb out onto the roof like I sometimes do, so I lean on the windowsill and focus my attention on the sky. On clear winter nights the constellation Orion hangs perfectly framed in my window, and beyond him a backdrop of sky dotted so dense with stars it looks like sugar spilled across the night. But right now I can't see any of them. Instead, the town lights reflect off the cloud-filled sky and it glows pale white, while fireplaces stream wood smoke into the air, leaving the night hazy around the edges.

A single snowflake twirls down onto the ledge of my window, and then another, and I watch as they melt almost instantaneously. Flurries like this aren't unheard of this late into spring. But storms are rare. Like the one Julianna Farnetti and Shane Cruz disappeared into. The way people tell it, that storm came fierce and unexpected, then was gone just as quickly.

I eye the envelope again and wonder if it started out with a whisper and a single flake, like this right now. I wonder if she wrote about trivial things like the weather in her journal. I probably would have for this assignment. It'd be a safe thing to write about, something that wouldn't matter if anyone else read it. Or maybe she didn't worry about that. Maybe she only wrote about Shane and what it was like to be in love. Maybe Julianna took the assignment to heart and put her truest self into words, like Kinney tells his seniors to do.

It's hard to guess without ever having known her. She was so much older than me, and lived in the seemingly distant world of high school. But even then I knew of her. She stood out to everyone, including my seven-year-old self. I'd seen her crowned queen at a homecoming football game, and after that, catching a glimpse of her around town was like seeing a real-life princess. The version of her in my memory is of the kind of girl I wanted to grow up to be. The version the town stories have painted of her is just as perfect—vibrant and full of life, special on her own, but exceptional together with Shane. And then there's the last version. The tragic one, of youth and innocence lost below the surface of a half-frozen lake. Maybe they're all true. Or maybe none of them are. People always put their own spin on things, remember what they want to remember, and somewhere in the middle of it all is the truth—the real version—one you could only write yourself if you were willing to.

I pick up the envelope and turn it over in my hands. This could be the real version right here. The one that might be more than the stories we've all heard and the labels she was given: homecoming queen, Shane's girlfriend, the next Cruz Wife. Perfect. Missing. Tragedy. Really, these are the only things I know about her. But I'm sure there's more. We're all more than the person we show to everyone else. At least I hope so. Because I *feel* like there's more to me than that. I just haven't had a chance yet to show it.

I set the envelope down and run my fingers over her name again. I wonder what things Julianna Farnetti kept for herself. What things she chose to write down or leave out. Maybe things she never had a chance to find out, or do, or be. If I think about it this way, it seems almost honorable to want to know who the real Julianna was. The girl behind the myth. It also gives me a reason to pick up the envelope again and slide my finger beneath the flap and the tape that has sealed it shut for a decade. When I do, the sound of it tearing away from the paper is the only audible thing in my room.

Carefully, I slide the black-and-white composition book out of the envelope, then turn it over in my hands. The edges of the pages aren't yellowed, like I expected. There's no musty smell to it. In fact it looks brand-new. Like it could've been written yesterday. The floor creaks on the other side of my closed door and startles me so much I nearly toss the journal out the window. It's nothing, though. Just my own guilt and the knowledge that if I actually open Julianna's journal, there's no undoing that act.

It makes my chest a little tight when I look down at it in my hands. Her name is written on the cover in the same loopy handwriting as the envelope, but over all the *i*'s are little spirals instead of dots. I run my fingers over the rounded corners, lift the front cover away from the pages, just barely, then let it fall back into place where it belongs. Then, for the second time today, I feel like what I'm about to do is wrong—but I do it anyway. The first page steals my breath. It's dated May 20.

Yesterday, ten years ago.

*May 20*

............

*"Tell me, what is it you plan to do*
*with your one wild and precious life?"*
*—MARY OLIVER*

*I love this. Mr. Kinney had it written on the board this morning when we came in. Once we all sat down, he read the words out loud in his booming voice.*

*"Tell me," he said, looking us over, "what is it you plan to do with your one wild and precious life? As seniors, this is relevant to you, isn't it? You're about to go out into the world and show it who you really are. What will you live for? Be passionate about? Define yourself by?"*

*He threw all of these big, rhetorical questions out, and no one said a thing, but I was thinking about it.*

*How do you begin to answer something like that?*

*"I want you to ponder these things," he said. "Don't just give them a fleeting thought—take a careful look at yourself now. Then think about the question some more:*

*What will you do with this one wild and precious life of yours? There really is only one."*

*He held up a handful of composition books as he went on. "So when the answers and ideas start coming to you, I want you to write them down in these.*

*"This is your last assignment in my class. You have from now until graduation day to write about who you are right now, who you want to be, what you want most— all of these things that will make up your one life."*

*He stepped to the first desk in my row and handed Jenna a stack of journals to pass back, then moved on to the next one. "Be idealistic, dream big—now's your chance. You can write as little or as much as you want. Draw pictures, compose poems, it doesn't matter. I won't ever see them, and you won't earn a grade. But this—this is your most important assignment. It's for you and nobody else. When you're finished, you'll seal your notebooks up, and I'll pack them away. And ten years from now, the lives you've imagined for yourselves will come back to you— in your own words."*

*I got goose bumps when he said that.*

*I love the idea of writing all these things down for ourselves to read later, but it's scary, in a way. How many people have gotten older and forgotten about the*

*things they hoped for and dreamed about when they
were young? Or given up without ever taking a chance,
or settled in life because it's easier, or they're scared, or
whatever other excuses? How many people need a reminder
of who they once were?*

*I don't ever want to be someone who needs to be reminded.
I want to be someone bold, who takes risks and has no
regrets. I want to have a life made of beauty and love and
chance.*

*I can't know exactly what my life will be ten years from
now. But whatever happens, when Kinney sends this
journal to me, I hope I recognize myself in it. And that I
see the beginning of something wild and precious, not some
sad reminder of what could have been.*

I close the book, wanting to take it back, what I've just
done. This trespass is too sad. Ironic in the worst possible
way, because I know how this story ends. I know the answer
to her question about where she would be. An image of
Julianna and Shane, suspended in the blue of Summit Lake,
crystallizes in my mind, her blond hair splayed wide around
her, her fingers entwined with his, both of them frozen in
time, forever young, just like on the billboard.

A shiver runs the length of my body, and I shove the
journal back into the envelope, then into my backpack. Zip
it up tight. Slowly, the idea that I still have a chance to do

the right thing untangles the knot of regret in my stomach. I know exactly what to do with her journal now. Tomorrow I will seal it up again and send it back to Julianna, like she was promised ten years ago. I won't need any address or postage. Just a drive out to Summit Lake and something with enough weight to sink it all the way to the bottom.

6.

"On the Heart's Beginning to Cloud the Mind"
—1934

When the phone rings before six a.m., I know there's no chance I'll be driving out to Summit Lake. It means last night's storm brought too much snow, too fast for the plows to have the roads cleared in time for the buses this morning. Which means no school either. I lie in the quiet dark of my room, relieved I don't have to get up anytime soon.

Julianna's words and my own guilt over reading them had run endless circles through my mind all night, keeping me floating in that strange, fitful space between sleep and consciousness. At some point the wind kicked up and the few flakes outside swirled together and multiplied until they became a solid wall of white that blasted my windows for what felt like hours. I took it as a sign that I'd somehow disturbed the balance of nature when I opened up that envelope. That's how Shakespeare would've written it, anyway.

Now, in the calm of the morning, it feels like everything could've been a dream—the scholarship, the envelope with her name on it, and the journal inside. I almost wish it was, so I could pull my covers tight around me and sleep through the day. Or just enjoy it without worrying about anything else.

When I was little, snow days like this meant pulling on my boots and snowsuit and heading out into the white freedom. While my mom went off to her shop to do inventory or payroll or ordering (because God forbid she take a day off), my dad would switch his computer off and join me outside to build an igloo or sled run or snowman. It never took any coaxing, as he was well into his "writer's block" stage by then and seemed to welcome any reason not to sit in front of his computer waiting for words to come to him. On those days we'd stay out in the snow until we were starving and our fingers and toes were numb, then come inside for tomato soup and grilled cheese, his snow day specialty.

Those days had a magic to them that I think came from him being free from the weight of expectation, and happy to be out in the fresh air with me, soaking up life instead of watching it from his office window. Until my mom would walk back through the door and see that he'd spent the day playing with me instead of writing his next award-winning poetry collection. Then the feeling would dissolve, and her silent disapproval would send him back to his office to "work," and me up to my room to "read," and we'd be back to the routine realities of life.

The knock at my bedroom door does the same thing. Before I can say *come in*, my mom does, bringing with her a cloud of perfume. Of course she's already dressed, made up, and accessorized. If you want to sell expensive clothes to tourists, you have to look the part, and she does, all in black with her dark hair pulled back into a low bun. She wears sophistication well.

"Parker, you awake? No school today. I'm going to walk over to the shop and get some inventory done. You want to come with? We could go over your speech some more. I had a few thoughts—did you get a lot done last night?" She stops talking long enough to take a sip from her leather-bound travel mug, then glances meaningfully at my desk.

"Yep," I lie, "I did." It's too early for the lecture I'll get if I tell her I haven't started yet.

Her face brightens and she steps fully into my room. "Want me to take a look at what you've got so far?"

"No, no, not yet," I say, too quickly. I hop out of bed and put myself between her and the desk, swooping up my Robert Frost book in the process. "It's really rough still. Mostly just notes. I'm actually thinking of working in a poem if I can." I hold the book up like a shield, hoping the Post-its sticking out from every direction are evidence enough I really have gotten started. "Dad has all the best ones marked in here."

Her smile falters, almost imperceptibly. "Oh. Well that's . . . good. That's fine."

Immediately, I feel guilty. I've just pushed a button I didn't mean to. The one where she somehow thinks I value his opinion over hers, like it's a competition. Poetry over pragmatism. "Actually," I add quickly, "I'm really excited, because I think I can find one that ties in perfectly with all the things *you* were talking about last night."

She clears her throat and ignores my attempt to smooth things over. "I put a roast in the Crock-Pot for dinner. Keep an eye on it and if the liquid gets too low, add a little broth. I'll be home around five."

"Okay," I answer. Without another word she steps back into the hall and reaches for the knob to close my door.

"Hey, Mom?" It surprises me when I stop her, but something in me wants to ask a question I thought about all night after reading Julianna's journal.

"Yes?" She raises her eyebrows expectantly.

I want to ask if she ever let go of something *she* dreamed of or hoped for. If she had things she used to want to be, or do, that she never got to. Instead I say, "It's sad that they died so young."

She gives me a quizzical look.

"Shane Cruz and Julianna Farnetti, I mean. They missed out on so much."

My mom's face softens a touch. "They did," she says, nodding. "It was very sad. And that's why the family offers the scholarship every year—to give other young people a chance at everything the two of them missed out on." She pauses and looks at my desk again. "Maybe *that's* something you should keep in mind as you write your speech. You deserve that chance, Parker. Work hard today, okay?"

"Of course," I answer. And I promise myself that I will.

The stillness of the house when I get out of the shower is both heavy and familiar. My mom's boutique has demanded her time as far back as I can imagine, so I'm accustomed to being at home alone. Lots of times, I actually prefer it. But this morning it's unsettling. Julianna's journal is still sitting right there in my bag, and no one in the world knows I have it. No one in the world would know if I opened it up and read more about who she was and what she wanted, and all the things she missed out on. But I can't, I tell myself. Or rather, I shouldn't.

What I *should* do, what I need to do, is actually get started on my speech. A week and a half isn't a lot of time to write something that so much depends on, so I sit down at my desk and turn on the computer. While it powers on I crack my window to let the fresh air in, and I light the vanilla candle on my desk, both of these things part of my work ritual. And then I take a deep breath, open a new document, and close my eyes a moment to focus. How to begin? A strong opening line. I open my eyes and the cursor blinks impassively on the blank page. I think of Julianna's handwriting.

*"Tell me, what do you plan to do*
*with your one wild and precious life?"*

I type the question and let it float there in black and white. Wonder for a moment what my most honest answer would be, if it were all up to me. Then I delete it and the blank page seems fitting. I really don't know.

Downstairs I pour a bowl of cereal and eat it at the counter in front of my mom's laptop. It's open to her e-mail, which I close before checking my own. Nothing. I try Facebook, hoping maybe Kat sent me one of her slightly inappropriate messages there. Again, nothing. Just for the heck of it I type Trevor Collins's name in the search box and click on his page when it comes up.

Apparently I'm not the only one awake early with time to kill. He's just added a new album entitled *Going Big*. I smile and open it, curious. It's all snowboarding photos, which makes sense. He's carved out his own path in the snow since he got here, one that'll take him around the world for competitions after we graduate.

In the first one he's in his race uniform, leaning hard into the mountain to make a turn at an obviously ridiculous speed. Following that is a shot of him holding up a trophy, eyes bright and cheeks red from the cold. I click on the next one and it literally takes my breath away.

It's of him impossibly high in the air, back arched against the blue of the sky, hand grasping his board behind him. The photo itself is impressive, but that's not what gets me. It's the expression on his face, a mix of intensity and pure love for what he's doing at that moment. It makes me wonder if I ever look like that doing anything. It really is impressive, and it's no wonder he's got sponsors lining up. And girls, for that matter. I click away quickly at the thought, like if I stay too long, he might be able to tell I've been there looking. Thinking about him.

I close the computer and sit back on the couch, restless. I don't know what to do with today, let alone my one wild and precious life.

Julianna seemed to, though.

I get up and climb the stairs to my room, justifying what I'm about to do with every step. And this time, when I sit on my bed with her journal in my hands, it's surprisingly easy to open it up.

*May 22*

............

*Mr. Kinney said he wants us to write about who we'll be in life, starting with who we are right now. Honestly, that seems like an impossible thing to do. I don't know if you can ever truly see yourself in the present. It's too close. It's easier to see who you were in the past. If I look back, I can see exactly who I was four years ago, before I met Shane.*

*I showed up here beyond shy, not trusting anyone, and scared of everything—from all the kids who seemed like they'd always known each other to having to start over when life as I knew it had just ended. I was an outsider in this school, with what felt like no chance of fitting in. The first day was the worst of my life at that point. I learned* what it meant to feel like I was utterly alone, to go an entire day without talking to anyone, to feel invisible. It's crazy to think, but I might've stayed that way, become a totally different person than I am now, if Shane hadn't seen me the next day. That was when I learned what it felt like to walk down the hallway with him by my side, and that changed everything.

I was late to school that day. He was too, and we met in the office. He asked if I was all right (I'd been crying), I said I was fine, he said I was a liar, and it made me smile. He walked me to class and I didn't protest, but I didn't speak, either, because he was so perfect. I didn't want to ruin it. When we got to the door, I didn't want to go in, and I could tell he didn't want to leave, but he said he'd find me at break, and he did. He was waiting for me outside of my next class, and we had our first date in the school cafeteria over undercooked cinnamon rolls and lukewarm hot chocolate.

He claims our first date was actually a few days later, when he brought me to the top of the mountain in a gondola and we ate Chinese food out of cartons and watched the lights from town twinkle below us while the stars spread out like tiny lights far above us. I remember that night too, because I felt like someone different. Better than who I was before.

But that first day we met is one of those things you look back on, and see, so clearly, that it was meant to be. He *saved me from being lost and out of place, and that's what he's been doing ever since. I showed up here in pieces. He put me back together.*

*He was the first person to really see me, and he's been my first everything since then.*

*My first kiss—in the rain, under an umbrella of pine trees, with the smell of the rain rising around us. My first "I love you," whispered soft as the snowflakes that fell all around a few months later. He's the first person I've given every bit of myself to, and the only person I've ever truly loved.*

*After four years we know each other's hearts and souls. We've grown and loved and fought and everything in between, which is why, to talk about who I am, I have to start with him. The person I am now, and who I want to be in the future, is wrapped up tight in Shane, and in us together.*

*I can't imagine it, or me, any other way.*

I close the journal, but the last line lingers. I can't imagine it any other way either, not at all. It's impossible to picture her the way she described herself before Shane, so scared and alone. I wonder, for a second, the same thing she did. Who would she have been if she hadn't met him that day?

Would her name have been one in the box that I passed over without a second glance? The things she wrote about in her journal, her entire life, might have been different. She might never have been any of the things she was with Shane. They might both still be alive instead of ghosts in our town.

As tragic as the end of their story is, I'm glad it started out this way. A real-life, meant-to-be love story. I don't want to stop reading. I flip through the pages, decide I could definitely finish it in a day, and make myself a deal: I can read it, but when I finish, I'll seal it back up and take it to Summit Lake. Back to Julianna, like I'd decided before. I won't talk about or show it to anyone. I'll act like it never existed.

## 7.

"I shall set forth for somewhere,
I shall make the reckless choice"
—*"THE SOUND OF TREES,"* 1916

My phone buzzes from my desk, startling me more than it should. I glance at the number before I pick it up. Kat, of course.

"Morning, sunshine. Little early for you to be awake on a day like today, isn't it?" I say.

She yawns. "Jesus, yes. I need some coffee."

"I thought you might say that." It's the perfect excuse for her to go stalk Lane some more.

"So meet me at Kismet," Kat says, like she's read my mind.

I glance down at the journal, weighing my options. "Maybe later. I'm kind of busy right now."

Kat's sigh comes over the phone like a gust of wind.

"Really? What are you busy with? Sitting in your sweats, watching *The Notebook*? She forgets who he is every time, P."

"Shut up." I laugh. "One of these days you're going to sit down and watch it with me and I guarantee you'll bawl your eyes out. It's *that* good."

"Whatever. So you'll meet me then? I have a plan. A brilliant plan that needs to be hashed out over coffee, with a view of Lane."

"A plan for what?"

"For our last hurrah before graduation. It came to me in a dream."

It's my turn for blatant sarcasm. "Really?"

"No. But it may as well have. It's *that* good. So just meet me over there in a half hour, okay?"

"Fine. I'll see you in a few." I hang up. Look around the room. So much for curling up with the journal and reading all day. Maybe it's better this way, though. I can make it last, stretch out the story instead of reading it all in one sitting. I'll go to the coffee shop and hear Kat's plan, which, just like all her others, will involve ten things I would never be allowed to do.

The trick will be talking without mentioning Julianna's journal. It's the kind of thing that Kat would die over, and the thought of her reaction alone is a huge temptation to say something. She wouldn't believe I'd found it. And she definitely wouldn't believe I'd actually taken it and read it. I almost don't believe I did either. I give it one last look, then slide it back into the envelope and put it under my bed, safe for later.

"Are you even listening to me?" Kat asks. We're sitting at the same table we did yesterday, drinking the same drinks, but this time the café is full of kids from school who have nothing better to do with the snow day. Between the hiss of the espresso machine, the voices of everyone all around me, and Julianna Farnetti's words in my head, I haven't really heard a thing Kat's said since we sat down.

"I *was* listening," I say. "Your plan has something to do with ditching school, lying to our moms, and me somehow avoiding being grounded for the rest of my life, right?" It's a guess, but those are usually the core elements of her schemes. I don't need to listen to know that. Instead, I'd been thinking about Julianna and Shane, and what it must've been like to be that wrapped up in each other.

"You were not listening," Kat says, taking a sip of her mocha and scanning for Lane. "If you were, you wouldn't have missed the part about this being the best plan I've ever come up with and you not being allowed to say no. Which means you're in by default now."

"Fine," I say, "whatever." I stir the contents of my mug into a spiral of whipped cream and chai. We've never actually carried out one of her plans, anyway. It's just talk.

"Really? You're in? What's wrong with you?"

"Nothing," I say. And it's true. Nothing's wrong, I just know she won't take no for an answer, so the best way to get back to my house and Julianna's journal is to go along with it. "So wait—what did I just agree to?"

A mischievous smile spreads across her face. "To ditching Senior Ditch Day next week, telling your mom you're staying at my house for the night, and then taking a little road trip with me instead." I nod, and she pauses before adding, "And possibly bringing Trevor Collins and Lane with us." Now she sits back, arms crossed over her chest, beaming at the genius of her plan.

I laugh. "Sure, yeah. That'll totally work. Nothing wrong with that plan at all."

"There's not." She shrugs. "Just depends on you having enough guts to actually do it. We won't get caught, but if we do, what's your mom gonna do at that point? Ground you from college?"

"Where would we go on this road trip?" I ask, just for fun.

"Anywhere." She leans forward on her elbows and grabs my hands. "That's the *point*, Parker. It'd be a couple days of freedom to get out of here and go wherever we want. Personally, I vote for the beach."

"What beach?"

"Oh my God. *Any* beach that we could drive to. Use your imagination." She drops my hands and sits back in her chair again. Takes a deep breath. "Come on. Say yes. You owe it to yourself and me to do this before you leave."

"It's not much of a plan—"

"It's a wide open plan. With room for possibilities. We can figure out the rest as we go."

I look at her, my best friend, and think of how, just like Shane with Julianna, a lot of who I am right now I owe to Kat. She's the one who pushes me out of my comfort zone when I let her, who forces me to do things I wouldn't have the guts to do when I don't, and who is always asking me her own version of the question Mr. Kinney put on the board for Julianna and her class. The same one I'd asked myself this morning.

"Maybe," I say finally. "But we'd have to figure out an *actual* plan first. Like with money, and a schedule, and maps."

Kat grins triumphantly. "Which is where you come in. That's the lame but necessary stuff you're good at, so it's perfect."

We spend the rest of the afternoon holed up in Kat's bedroom, planning our last-ditch senior trip, which I still don't really see us taking. I search every beach we can make it to and back from in two days. She looks through magazines and picks out scandalous clothes and tiny bikinis for us to bring. I compare motel prices at every one of the beaches I find, and she plans how we'll get the boys to come along, and where we can all get fake IDs. By the time I get home, our plan has us leaving the day the rest of the senior class ditches to go float the river south of town and driving up the coast to San Francisco for a night out before we come back home the next day and my mom has not the slightest clue that I was out of town. Seizing the day. Sure.

When I walk through my door and stomp the snow off my boots, the same quiet from before greets me. It's past five, when she said she'd be home, but Mom is still gone at her shop, or maybe having a drink with Lucy, who's her grown-up version of Kat, and who's going through a nasty divorce for the third time around. I turn up the thermostat, slide out of my coat, and think maybe Kat was right. Maybe my mom wouldn't notice at all if I left for a day, or even two. Except the scholarship reception is so close I know she'll be in hyper-preparation mode, which would be the biggest problem to get around. I'd have to have my speech written, practiced, and in the bag for her to even consider letting me stay at Kat's the weekend before.

In the kitchen the roast in the Crock-Pot looks overdone and unappetizing, so I settle on my second bowl of cereal today, this one eaten standing in the kitchen. I eat fast, because I don't have any time to waste. I need to get started tonight, for sure. No more putting it off. I repeat this to myself all the way up the stairs to my room. But once I change, and light my candles, and settle in, it's not with my own words.

*May 23*

............

*Shane and I skipped seventh period today and drove out of town, down to the creek where we could tangle ourselves together under the sun and sky and forget the rest of the world existed. "I miss you," he whispered into my neck. I watched the aspen leaves dance above me in the breeze that kissed as much of my bare skin as he did, and then I closed my eyes and answered back without any words. After, we lay there for a long time, watching the clouds drift by, listening to the sound of the trees, and feeling the freedom of being just us together.*

*I've missed him too. Lately it seems like I've been fighting the pull of everyone else for him. His friends, who have this sudden renewed need to hang out every weekend at the same parties we've been going to since freshman year. He can't tell them no, so we go, but a night spent watching them play quarters isn't really time together. Then there's baseball, which he loves, and watching him play is fine, but I don't count it as being together either.*

*The biggest pull is his family though. They're a whole other journal entry on their own. It's a given that being a Cruz comes with a lot of expectations, but being the girlfriend of one seems to have just as many. I love them dearly, and I know how important they are to him. And they already treat me like I'm one of them, like it's settled that we'll be together, which is amazing and so sweet. Being with Shane and becoming a part of his family are probably the most perfect things I could ask for. But sometimes I wish he was just any guy instead of next in line for the whole mountain empire. He'd have more freedom in life that way. We'd have more freedom.*

*I've never asked, but I wonder—if he actually had a choice between going straight into what they've got planned for him and doing something completely different, which would he choose? It doesn't matter, I guess. He'd be crazy not to choose the life that's right in front of him. Just like I would be.*

*Today, under the trees and a sky we watched turn from blue to gold, we chose each other over everything else, and that's what really matters. We followed the trail past the Grove, where everyone carves their initials into the thin bark on the aspens, and hopped across the rocks in the creek to our own secret clearing where Shane carved ours when we were freshmen, holding hands and stumbling through the trees together.*

*It was the day he first told me he loved me, and I was so surprised I couldn't say anything back in that moment. Then when I finally pulled him in close and whispered that I loved him too, he smiled and said, "I know that." And he showed me the tree he'd already carved our initials into. It sounds silly, but I remember thinking how they'd always be there, no matter what. How, even long after we're both gone, there will be some little memory that we were once there, just the two of us, and that we were happy.*

I shut the journal and try to picture them as freshmen, laughing and weaving their way through the aspens to the tree Shane had carved their initials into. Saying I love you for the first time. And then, four years later, still going back to that same place together when they needed to get away from everything else. I wonder where the spot was. Is. If maybe their tree is still there, near the Grove, but separate from the rest of the marked-up trees. I've been there a few times, passed them all and thought how the random names and the graffiti-like carvings looked crude and ugly on the trees. For some reason, though, it seems to me that Shane and Julianna's names would be more like a memorial. More like a beautiful scar.

I wonder if, after all these years, it might still be there.

## 8.

"A Serious Step Lightly Taken"
*—1942*

It's early and the hall is mostly empty. Julianna's journal is safe in my backpack, my place now marked with my folded-up scholarship letter. The irony of having the journal of the girl the scholarship is named for hasn't escaped me, and I'm starting to think maybe it's fated somehow, that I have both. I shove my shaky hands in my pockets. Take a deep breath to ready myself for what I'm about to do. Then I walk into Mr. Kinney's classroom, as casually as I can.

He looks up from a stack of essays and nods at me. "Morning, Parker. I didn't get a chance to ask the other day—how'd you do with the journals?"

"Huh? Oh. Fine," I manage. "But, um . . ." I hesitate, scared.

But now is my chance if I'm going to do it. "I think . . . I think I may need to go to the database at the town library to find some of the addresses. There were a lot I couldn't find, and the school blocks so many sites . . ." I stop. It sounds less believable out loud than it did in my mind. Mr. Kinney is frowning down at an essay, red pen poised to scribble something in the margin. Apparently only half listening.

It gives me courage. I clear my throat. "Mr. Kinney?"

"I'm sorry, Parker," he says, looking up. "These freshman essays are a sad, sad lot for this point in the year. It's like they've forgotten everything I taught them." He puts his pen down and takes his glasses off. Looks at me with his full attention. "Anyway. What was your question?"

My words come out fast, smashed together in one nervous rush. "Oh—just that I need an off-campus pass for this period, and maybe next, so I can go through the city database for the journal addresses."

It's quiet for a few seconds, and I'm not sure he understood what I just said. He scrunches his brows together. I panic. *Oh my God. He knows. He knows I just lied and now I'm going to be in huge trouble and disappoint the teacher I respect most out of everyone, not to mention be reamed by my mom for trying to get away with something like this.*

"Sure," he says after too long a moment. "Why don't I write it for the rest of the week, just in case? That way you can take care of the postage and sending them off, too."

"Really?" *Shut up now. Don't sound so surprised.* "I mean, thank you. That's . . . that's perfect."

I watch as he pulls the slip out and signs and dates it for

the rest of the week, every first period. "Thank *you*, Parker," he says, tearing it off the pad and handing it to me. "It's a big favor you're helping me out with. I appreciate it. And so will all those kids when they get their journals back."

"It's really no problem." I smile, hoping to hide the twinge of guilt that tugs at my conscience, and wonder if he even remembers that this batch of journals belonged to Julianna and Shane's class. Or maybe he just decided not to mention it. Mr. Kinney goes back to his essays and I turn to go, marveling at the fact that it really had been no problem to get the pass. Simple. Like nothing. And now I'm free every morning for the rest of the week—

"Parker, wait," Mr. Kinney says. I freeze. Hold my breath. "Don't you need the journals?"

"I guess I probably do, huh?" I laugh—at my instant panic and at the fact that I'd completely forgotten about all of the other journals.

He hands me the heavy box from behind his desk. "Here you go. Good luck."

"Thanks," I say, backing toward the door this time, box in hand. As soon as he sits back down in his chair, I turn and practically make a run for it. I'm *ditching*—well, not technically, since it's excused, but it's the closest I've ever come, and the thought both exhilarates and slightly terrifies me at the same time.

When I make it down the hallway without any alarms going off, I let a tentative but proud smile creep onto my face. I feel good. Bold. Like Kat. I have to find her and tell her. Then convince her to ditch with me, which will be the easy part. The hard part will be getting her to drive down to the Grove and then go tromping around through the trees without telling her what I'm looking for. The only excuse I've come up with so far is to say I've had an epiphany of the carpe diem variety and want to go on an adventure. Just get out of school and town for a little bit. It's shaky, but it could work.

I haven't completely made up my mind *not* to tell her about the journal yet, but I'm not sure she'll understand at this point. I couldn't fall asleep last night until I'd decided to go find Shane and Julianna's tree. It doesn't totally make sense to me, why I need to see it so much, but I can't ignore it. Especially now that I know the story behind the carving. It's more evidence that love like theirs actually happens beyond books and movies, in real life. Life that's close to home.

As silly as it seems, it makes me feel like I somehow have a connection to it. To them. I want to see their tree the same way people want to see things that once were connected to famous people—especially once they're gone. Little slivers of their personal pasts, like photos no one has ever seen, or letters that surface years after their deaths. Or journals. Maybe because these are the things that somehow make them more real to us. Or maybe because all of them add to the myth of the person. It's hard to say which, but I need to find that tree, even if it takes me all week.

When I round the corner to Senior Hall, it's empty except for one person. Trevor Collins. Of course. My newfound boldness wavers the tiniest bit when I pass him and catch the mix of laundry detergent and the cologne he always wears that I always want to ask about so I can buy it for my future boyfriend. It's clean and sexy with a little bit of spice to it, which is how I imagine him to be. The future boyfriend, not Trevor. I know him well enough to know better than to imagine him that way. I don't say anything when I pass, but go straight to my locker, set the box of journals down, and spin the dial like I don't notice him there. That's when I feel him turn and look me over.

"Morning, Frost." He says it like he knows I'm pretending not to see him, which I'm sure he does.

"Oh, hey." I glance over, still trying to keep up the appearance that I'm surprised to see him there, then roll my eyes at myself as I push the lock up and open my locker. Where is Kat when I need her? It's so much easier talking to him with her around to hide behind. I pull out a binder I don't need, since I'm not going to class, and a stack of papers comes out with it and flutters to the ground. *Perfect.* Now I look as idiotic as I feel. I bend to pick them up and hide the blush I can feel creeping up my neck.

"Heard you're up for the big money," he says. I wait a second for an indecent offer to celebrate together in the art supply closet, but it doesn't come. Instead, he comes over and crouches down to help me with my mess. Close. Close enough for me to also smell the cinnamon gum he's chewing, and long enough for me to think it's sweet and that maybe he does have a bit of chivalry to him after all.

"Congratulations on that. That's pretty damn impressive." He smiles, and somewhere in me something melts a little, because that smile is pretty damn impressive too. Before I can remind myself that it's my turn to speak, he hands me the stray papers, then stands up. Waits for me to say something back.

"Oh, um . . . thanks. Congratulations on your snowboarding trophy."

Trevor looks confused.

*Oh my God, I need to shut up right now.*

"I mean, I saw some pictures . . ." *That were probably taken months ago, during the actual season, but that you put up yesterday . . . and now I'm a stalker.* Trevor cocks his head, eyebrow raised. *God help me.*

"Never mind," I manage.

He starts to say something, but God, in the form of Kat's voice, interrupts. "Hey!"

I turn around way too eagerly at the sound of her voice, and she greets me with a signature butt slap. "Today's the day you're going to ditch first with me, I feel it. Just like I feel like a mocha with a view of my favorite baristo."

A bemused smile breaks over Trevor's face as he looks from me to Kat, and back again. I want to turn and run. "Sounds like you've got places to go," he says. "Don't let me keep you."

Kat doesn't bother to keep a straight face. "You can come if you want. I don't want to interrupt whatever you guys have going on right here."

I fight the urge to kick her. And then flee.

Trevor laughs a little, shakes his head. "Thank you, but I think I'll leave the mochas and baristos to you ladies today."

He looks at me with clear blue eyes I could honestly dive right into if things were different. "You know, Frost, if you ever wanna see more than just Facebook pictures, I'm all yours."

"I . . ." I sputter, grasping at the last shreds of my dignity. "That's great of you, thanks," I say flatly. *Someone kill me now.*

Trevor hits me with a smile that's all confidence, then turns and walks—no, swaggers—down the hall, and I die right there. A slow, mortifying death.

"God, that boy smells good," Kat says, watching him. When he rounds the corner, she turns back to me. "So, what was that about? You're all red and flustered." She smiles. "Or is that hot and bothered?"

"Shut up," I say, trying to block the whole exchange from my consciousness.

She grins. "He just asked you out."

I bend down and grab one last paper from the floor without answering.

"*What?*" she asks innocently. "He did."

"That wasn't asking me out. That was him being completely full of himself." I close my locker and take a deep breath. "Besides. If he really were going to—which I would say no to—he should at least figure out how to do it without sounding like an ass. Or like he's doing me a favor."

"Sorry to break it to you, P, but actual guys don't talk like the ones in Nicholas Sparks books. And—I'm sure he'd happily do you a *few* favors if you wanted him to."

I roll my eyes. "I'm sure he would. And then the chase would be over and he wouldn't be interested anymore.

Which is why it can never happen. It's better this way."

"God, you're impossible."

"That's kind of the point. Now let's go get coffee."

She cocks her head. "*Really*? You realize the bell's about to ring, right?"

"Yeah." I shrug, like ditching class with her is something I've agreed to plenty of times. "But there's somewhere we have to go after. And you can't ask me any questions about it, okay?"

"Anywhere you want, P." She smiles. "I like this new you, whoever she is."

9.

"The Lesson for Today"
*—1942*

"The Grove? Why?" Kat asks, as she backs out of Kismet's parking lot. Lane's not working this morning, and Josh was especially untalkative, so it wasn't hard to convince her to take our drinks to go. This way we can hopefully make it back by break and I can go to third period. "Now that you ditched your first class you wanna go down to the creek and get high in the trees, too?"

"No, I just wanted to do something different today. You said you were sick of the snow." I look out the windshield at the remnants of yesterday's storm, now pushed to the sides of the road and already blackened by gravel and exhaust. "It probably didn't even stick down there. It might actually feel like spring." I pause, waiting to see if that'll be enough to get her to go. "Let's just go see. I don't want to go back to school yet."

"Okay," Kat says, hitting the gas hard enough that her tires squeal. I squeal too, but Kat just grins. "The Grove it is."

We blow out of town in her little red pickup with the windows down and the music up. Passing the COME AGAIN! sign at the edge of town when I should be in second period sends a giddy wave through me that I think I could get used to. The sun is out, the sky is brilliant blue in every direction, and the wind in my hair feels like freedom long overdue.

"So what are we *really* doing right now?" Kat yells over the wind and the music. "Because you realize this is *way* out of the realm of normal behavior for you." She turns the music down a bit.

Now would be the perfect time to tell her about the journal. She might totally get what we're doing driving out here in search of their initials. But if she knew, she'd definitely have to read it, and as much as I love her, I also know that she has a tendency to not keep things like this to herself. And since I stole it, I'm still a little protective of it, and myself, so I decide it's not time yet.

"What?" I ask. "Is it so bad that after almost eighteen years of you trying to get me to do things your way, I'm finally caving a little?" She looks at me like she knows I'm full of it. "Okay, fine." I fly my arm out the window, letting my hand dip and rise over invisible waves of air. "You said I had to do something unexpected. This is unexpected, right?"

"It's also random. But okay, I get it. You're not ready to tell me whatever it is yet." She shrugs. "It's fine. I can wait you out. Like I said before, you're a shitty secret keeper, anyway." She winks, then turns the music back up and cranks the wheel at the same time, sending us off the highway and onto the dirt road that leads out to the Grove, and I know she's probably right. I won't be able to keep this from her for long. It'd be like trying to fight fate.

I'd never be able to find the Grove without Kat, but I know it's hidden somewhere in the green vein of aspen trees on the hills in the distance. It's a big party spot for kids at our school, and always has been, from what I've heard— and now read. And it makes sense. It's just far enough out of town that it doesn't get near as much snow, but still close enough to make it worth the drive if you don't mind standing around in a clearing next to a creek to drink your beer. Which is both small-town *and* cliché, but that's just the way some things are. I haven't ever actually been to a party down here, seeing I've always had the earliest curfew of anyone and know better than to come out. Getting back before my mom called out the search party would be next to impossible, no matter how many times Kat promised me she'd do it.

But Kat knows the way well, and in a few minutes we turn off the wide, muddy road onto a narrower one that's rutted and littered with boulders every few feet. I wonder briefly if it's part of the actual creek and if it's the best idea to be driving through it, but Kat seems to know what she's doing. She downshifts or something—I don't know what—and I feel the tires grab the road a little more. We slow to a crawl to get over a rock the size of one of her tires, and Kat grips the steering wheel with more concentration than I've seen her use for most anything. When we bump over the rock and come down hard, all of a sudden I'm nervous. This is a bad idea, I'm sure of it now.

"Everything okay?" I ask.

"Yeah, but I don't know if we're gonna be able to make it all the way out there. It's not usually this rough. I don't want to get—"

Before she can finish the tires hit a thick patch of mud and I feel us lose traction. "Shit," Kat mutters. She jams her foot into the gas pedal to make it through, but that only makes it worse. The engine revs up to a high-pitched whine and our back tires spin, splattering mud out behind us in two big rooster tails.

"Kat, stop! You're making it worse."

She lets off the gas and smacks the steering wheel. "Shit, shit, shit. I thought I could make it."

I don't say anything. She shuts off the engine. When we both get out, my shoes squish into the same mud the back wheels of her truck are sunk into, deep.

"Maybe we can like, wedge something under it?" I offer. I have no idea.

Kat walks around the back, squishing every step of the way, and shakes her head. "I don't think so." She laughs. "We're screwed. Look at that." I do, and she's right. The back tires have spun themselves into two deep ruts that have already filled in with mud.

"Crap, this is all my fault. I'm so, so sorry." I feel awful for a few seconds. And then I panic. "Oh my God. If my mom finds out about this she's going to freak. Seriously. We have to get the car out and get back before she knows I'm not in school."

I look around for something to wedge under the back tires to give them traction—a log, a rock, anything. "Maybe I can push it out." I've heard of people getting superhuman strength in dire situations, which this all of a sudden is. Kat just looks at me like I'm being stupid, which might be the case, but I don't know what else to do at the moment.

"*What?*" I ask. "You get in and give it some gas, and I'll push." I say it with confidence, then roll up my sleeves, step into the mud, and put my hands on the bumper, ready to get the truck out and save my butt from being grounded for the rest of senior year.

"It's not gonna work," she says flatly.

"Well, we have to try something. This can't happen. I can't get caught the very first time I ditch. That's ridiculous."

I wonder for a second if the desperation in my voice is as obvious to Kat as it is to me, and then I know it is, because she twists her long hair up into a bun, walks back to her open door, and gets in. "Don't get pissed if you get dirty, because you will." She closes her door, then turns the key, and the engine jumps to life again. "Okay," she yells back to me. "You ready? Push on three!"

"Okay!" I dig the heels of my hands into the bumper and try to find something in the mud to brace my feet against.

"One . . . two . . ."

"Go easy at first," I yell, but it's too late.

"Three!" She hits the gas hard, sending a mud explosion flying from both tires. In the half second it takes for me to squeeze my eyes shut and try to remember to push, it splatters my face and my feet slip out from under me like something out of a cartoon. And that's probably what I look like, lying face-first in the mud when she shuts the truck off.

By the time Kat gets back to me, I'm on my hands and knees wiping grit from my mouth and she's laughing so hard she can't talk or breathe. I chuck a handful of mud at her, which only makes her laugh more, then she loses her balance and ends up on her butt right next to me, and now it's my turn to laugh so hard I can't breathe. She grabs a handful of mud and smears it down my arm. I glop some onto her leg. We sit there in the mud like that for I don't know how long, laughing until tears stream down our faces and it's one of those moments I want to always remember. One that years from now will make me laugh just to think about. It makes me miss Kat already.

Finally, I catch my breath. "I'm sorry. This is totally my fault."

Kat nods slowly, traces a shape in the mud. "Yep," she says. "Which means now you have to tell me what we're doing here with my car stuck in the mud and you about to get your ass handed to you by your mom." She's right, and she knows it. I owe her an explanation, which she waits for with a smug smile on her face.

"Fine," I say. "But you're gonna think it's stupid."

"Try me."

"Okay." I take a deep breath. "I heard that Shane Cruz's and Julianna Farnetti's initials were carved into a tree out here near the Grove, and I wanted to see if I could find them." It's the truth, just not the whole thing.

Kat's quiet a moment. "You're kidding, right? Their initials on a *tree* is why we're here? Do you know how many initials are carved into the trees down there?"

"I told you you'd think it was stupid—"

"I don't know if stupid's the right word," she says, getting to her feet. "But it is kind of weird. Why are you all of a sudden obsessed with them since you got that letter? It's not like you get points with the scholarship board for finding their lost initials."

"I don't know, I . . . it's kind of romantic to think they're out here somewhere. I just wanted to see."

Kat shakes her head. "Clearly, you're in need of a life outside of sappy books and movies," she says. "And a guy. Which I'm gonna help you out with right now. I know how you like your knights in shining armor, so let's call one to come get us out of this mess."

"Who?"

"I don't know. Whoever's willing to drive all the way out here and get us unstuck. Relax about it," she says with a wink. "Enjoy the sun and the last of your freedom."

# 10.

"He asked with the eyes more than the lips . . ."
—*"LOVE AND A QUESTION," 1913*

By the time we finally hear an engine heading our way, the sun is high and the mud on our clothes is nearly dry, and I'm grimly resigned to the fact that I probably won't be leaving my house for anything but school for the rest of the year. It doesn't matter though. This turned out to be such a bad idea, I don't even care.

And then I do care. Because when our rescue car rounds the turn, I can see it's actually a silver Suburban—one that I know well. I look at Kat and shake my head without saying anything.

"*What?*" she asks innocently, but her smile says she knows exactly what.

"You called Trevor Collins to come get us?" I wipe at my face, try to smooth my mud-caked hair. "That's your idea of a knight in shining armor?"

Kat just smiles, proud of herself, then shrugs. "Don't be so surprised. Who did you think I was gonna call? I knew he'd come if I told him I was with you. Turns out I was right. Just like always."

The Suburban stops, then does a three-point turn before backing up to Kat's bumper. When Trevor gets out, it's with a smug grin on his face, one that's aimed right at me. "You could've just called me and said you wanted to hang out, Frost. No need to go to all this trouble."

"Well, you know," I say rubbing at a patch of mud on my forearm. "I figure when you're up against such a long list of people vying for your attention, it's better to take a different approach."

"Took you long enough," Kat says.

Trevor walks around to the back of his car and opens the door, leans in, and comes back out with a rope. "I would've come sooner if I'd known mochas and baristos were code for mud-wrestling." He squats down to the truck and, with hands that look sure and strong, knots the rope around Kat's bumper and then his own. Then without another word, he hops back in his car, hits the gas, and pops Kat's truck out of the mud like it's nothing.

Kat nudges me with her elbow. "He's taking you home."

"No."

"*Yes.*" She smiles through her teeth, then hooks an arm through mine and drags me over to the bumpers, where

Trevor is now untying the rope. "Yay, thank you!" She gushes. "We owe you big-time for that." She pauses, and I realize a second too late I should've probably added something.

"It's fine," he smiles. "Any excuse to get out of sixth period." He holds one end of the rope and quickly loops the rest of it around his elbow. "What were you guys doing out here, anyway?"

"Nothing," I say, right at the same time Kat practically shoves me forward.

"Parker can tell you all about it on the way home. You don't mind giving her a ride, do you?"

"Sure. No problem." Trevor looks from Kat to me. "You ready?"

Kat smiles sweetly at me, and I'm left powerless against her.

"Um . . . let me just go get my bag." And a little courage, and maybe a spritz of perfume and a mint or something. I'm sure I smell awesome after my mud bath.

When I get in, the inside of Trevor's car does smell awesome. And it's immaculate—not an empty gum wrapper or stray penny anywhere, which makes me all the more conscious of my muddy clothes sitting in the front seat. And of how close we are. And of how awkwardly quiet it is all of a sudden as we work our way back to the main highway. It's easy to quip back and forth in the hall with Kat around, but alone together in his car is a different story. I am quipless. But he is too, it seems.

I clear my throat. "Thanks. That was really nice of you to drive all the way out there for us. We would've been stuck out there forever otherwise."

"No problem." He glances over at me. "So . . . do I get to know what you guys were doing out there?"

"I was looking for something."

"Oh. That's specific."

"It was stupid. You don't wanna know what it was."

"No, now I don't at all," he says.

We drive in silence for thirty seconds that feels like it's stretched out into thirty minutes. "Okay," I say, unable to handle the quiet any longer. "You know Shane Cruz and Julianna Farnetti?"

"You mean them?" He points, and I look up in time to see the billboard coming up on the shoulder. I hadn't thought of it for a long time before yesterday. I don't think most people do anymore. That's just how it goes with the things you see every day. Eventually they start to fade into the background. But now that her journal is in my backpack, and the snow has melted, their pictures are visible again beneath the foggy plexiglass. I see them in a whole new light.

"Yes, them," I say. I keep my eyes on Julianna as we get closer, can't take them off of her, actually. In my memory she's older, and much more grown up than me. But in her senior picture on the billboard, she looks young, like she could be anyone in my class. And she could've. I'm the same age as she was when she died. The same age as she was when she wrote on those pages of the journal that's sitting in my backpack on the floor of Trevor's car right now. I keep my eyes on her even as we pass by, sad for her all of a sudden because I think again of that first line on that first page. The place where I'm at in life, that feels like the beginning of everything, was the end for her. For a moment it makes me sadder than it should.

"What about them?" Trevor asks, pulling me back.

"Oh—I, um, I heard somewhere that their initials are carved into one of the trees out there, and I wanted to go find them. I don't know why. It's stupid."

Trevor shrugs. "It's not that stupid. They're kind of like cult figures around here. Town history. I get it."

"I've never thought of them as cult figures, but I guess it's true, in a way. I think because everyone remembers when they disappeared." We pass the billboard and I watch the road. "My dad was on the search party that went out for them the day after they crashed, and I have this vivid memory of him coming home after. He was standing in the kitchen, telling my mom the whole thing about how they found the Jeep upside down at the bottom of the ravine near the river and how the bodies must've gotten swept right into Summit Lake. I didn't know what bodies they were talking about until the next day, when everyone knew, and there was the candlelight vigil, and . . ." I realize the car has slowed way down and Trevor seems to be only half listening. "I'm sorry. You probably didn't need to hear the *entire* story." *God, why can I not just have a normal conversation with him?*

"No, it's fine," he says. "That's the most you've ever said to me, so I was gonna let you keep going." He smiles over at me. "I was just trying to figure out where you want me to take you. It's still seventh period, so . . ." He looks me over, and I feel his eyes on every mud-covered inch of me. "You probably wanna go home though, right? To shower?"

"Yeah, that'd be good." I pinch my crusty shirt away from my chest and a few flecks of mud fall off onto my legs. I see Trevor see them. "Oh, crap, I'm sorry. I'm totally getting your car dirty."

He smirks, but doesn't say anything.

"*What?*" I fight the urge to check the mirror. Do I still have dirt in my teeth? Mud stuck in my nose?

"Nothing, don't worry about it." His eyes slide over to me for a second before they bounce back to the road and he shakes his head. "I wasn't looking at the mud, Frost."

## 11.

"On Looking Up by Chance at the Constellations"
*—1928*

By the time my mom walks through the door, I've showered, erased the message from the school about my unexcused absences for periods two through seven, and am still giddy at the fact that I somehow got away with my little foray out onto the edge today. And it was fun. And Trevor Collins was checking me out in his car.

I've even got a pot of spaghetti boiling on the stove, but it's more a gesture than anything else, because my mom probably won't eat any. Instead, she'll pour a glass of wine and sit down at her computer to check her e-mail even though she just came from work. There's an ebb and flow to her store, which caters to the high-end tourist ladies who want to shop while everyone else skis. The store lives and dies by November through January. Spring, summer, and fall are the slow times, which means she'll stress out at the end of every month until things pick back up next ski season.

"Hey, Mom," I say as she sighs her way into the kitchen. "Long day?"

"You have no idea." She stands on tiptoe, reaching in the cabinet for a wine glass. "Sales for spring break were *not* what I was hoping for. Not even close. At this rate I may actually have to cut down hours come September."

"You say that every May, and by every September, it's fine. You always make it." I heft the pot over to the sink and stand back from the billow of steam when I dump the noodles in the strainer. "You want some spaghetti?"

She shakes her head. "Not now. I may have some later." It's quiet a moment as I scoop some into a bowl for myself, add a ladle of sauce, and grab the parmesan cheese. "So," she says, making a point to look at me. "How was your day?"

A little tremor of nervousness zips through my stomach, but I shake the parmesan can over my bowl and play it cool. "Fine."

She nods. "Good." Then she pours her wine and sits down at the table with her laptop. When she doesn't ask about anything else, not even my speech, it surprises me. Normally she doesn't let it go at just that, which means things at the shop must be really bad.

Partly because I don't want to spend my dinner in silence, and partly because I'm nervous, I elaborate. "I've been helping Mr. Kinney with these senior journals he sends out every year, so that's pretty cool." She nods absently, alternately scrolling and tapping. "They're from ten years ago, and now we're mailing them out to the people who wrote them. It's sort of like a personal time capsule of who they were when they were seniors." I twirl my fork until it's full and take a bite of spaghetti.

She looks up for a second. "Hm. I wouldn't want to read anything I wrote about when I was seventeen."

"Why?"

"Oh, it'd just be embarrassing to read all the things I thought were *so* important back then. Life is different once you grow up. Not so dramatic. By the time you're my age you'll get it." She pauses, and swirls the wine in her glass, thinking. "I would just hate to look back and see how naive I'd been about a lot of things. Life works out a lot differently than you can ever imagine at seventeen."

She stops herself and I shovel another tightly wrapped bundle of spaghetti into my mouth. The only sound is the clink of my empty fork when I rest it on the bowl. We both know what she just said without actually saying it. When I was old enough to do the math I figured out why my parents had gotten married. When I got brave enough to ask her about it, she sat me down and told me all the things a parent is supposed to say: that yes, I was a surprise to her and my dad, and so they did what they thought was best back then and got married, and even though they weren't the right people for each other, I was the best surprise either one of them had ever gotten.

That was years ago, and for the most part she's always

been good at maintaining that glass-half-full version. But sometimes, in little moments like this, she slips. And this slip makes me wonder what it was she would've dreamed of doing at seventeen. It probably wasn't running a boutique that somehow squeaks by every year in a town she never really wanted to live in to begin with, while raising a daughter mostly by herself.

"I didn't mean anything by that, Parker. I just . . . I'm a little stressed about the store right now." She takes a deep breath and recomposes her smile. "Anyway, I'm sure Mr. Kinney appreciates your help with those. It must be quite a production to find all of the addresses and get them sent out."

"It is." I smile. "I actually have a few to look up tonight. I should get back to it." I'm not hungry anymore, so I get up, put the bowl in the sink, and kiss my mom on the top of her head to let her know I didn't take what she said personally.

She smiles relief and rubs a hand on my back. "Don't let this project take over everything else. Your number one priority right now should be your speech. It's coming along?" I nod and she pats me on the back. "Good. I can't wait to read it when you're ready. I love you, Parker."

"Love you too, Mom." I give her shoulder an extra squeeze, then leave her at the table with her sales figures, cabernet, and all the things she would have done differently.

Upstairs in my room I bring my mind back to the day's adventure and the feeling of freedom that came along with doing something risky. Ditching class is not a big deal to probably 99 percent of people. It was a little thing, deciding to do it. But it felt big at the same time, and between that and what my mom just said, I've got this tiny pang of regret when I think of how much I have probably missed out on in the last few years because I was too scared to take a risk, or too shy to speak up, or too worried to be bold. It is my one wild and precious life, after all.

And Shane and Julianna are proof that it could end at any moment. I know it was silly to go looking for their initials today, and I didn't really expect to find them, but I wanted to see them, not just read about them. I wanted proof that Shane and Julianna had been there, together and in love from the start. It doesn't matter that I know how it ends. My favorite part of any love story is the beginning. Like Romeo convincing Juliet to kiss him, a perfect stranger, at the ball. Or Noah climbing up the Ferris wheel to ask Allie out in *The Notebook*. Beginnings are magical.

And in books and movies they're magical in a way real life never is. So for the third night in a row, I don't do what I should. I don't sit down at my desk and start my speech. Instead, I open the window to let the cool night air in, light my candles, and get Julianna's journal out.

*May 24*

............

*"One often meets her destiny on the road
she takes to avoid it."*
*—Fortune cookie wisdom*

*It's such a tiny thing, a glance. That half second when eyes meet, lock, and before you can look away, there's <u>something</u>. A spark, a flash, I don't know what to call it. But it happened tonight when I walked through Shane's front door and into the party he wasn't supposed to be throwing. The usual mix of people from school and workers from the mountain filled all three floors of his house, but I saw someone new right away, standing alone in the middle of them all. He was tall, with wavy brown hair and eyes that stopped mine and held them there in the middle of a sea of familiar faces and shifting glances. And it was there. A pull, like gravity.*

*I looked away, and before I could look back, Shane was stumbling over to me in full life-of-the-party mode, beyond drunk and already apologizing for inviting half the town over when it was supposed to be just the two of us. And that's when it happened again, right over his shoulder, and for a second I lost what he was saying to me in the space between the unfamiliar brown eyes across the room and my own. And then they looked away again. And I was back.*

*Back to Shane's apologies and back to being disappointed because the night wasn't what I expected and I knew how it would go from there. He would drink more, talk louder, make jokes, and everyone would love it but me. I didn't say much, which only made him apologize more. Beg me to stay. Pull me in close, slide a hand around my waist, and kiss me with a mouth that tasted like beer and pot. And all of a sudden, I was done.*

*"Why do you want me to stay so bad?" I asked. "You have a whole houseful of people here to adore you."*

*"For later. When they're all gone." He winked, and tried to kiss me again, but I stepped back. If I'd been as drunk as he was, maybe I would've kissed him back, but I spun around to leave right then.*

*He caught my wrist, face pleading. "Wait, wait. I'm sorry. That was a joke. It was an asshole thing to say. I'm sorry. Just stay . . . please?"*

*I don't know why I didn't leave. I wanted to. I probably should've. But I didn't, and now a tiny part of me is glad. Because after I promised I'd stay, and Shane went back to the party, I stepped though the sliding glass door onto the balcony, and the guy with those eyes was out there, elbows leaned against the railing, staring up at the moonless sky.*

*It startled me, to see him there, but he just turned to me and smiled. "You know . . . sometimes we meet our destiny on the road we take to avoid it."*

*"Excuse me?"*

*"It was in my fortune cookie today." He took a step toward me, then motioned at the party inside. At Shane in the center of it. "You looked like you were*

*trying to avoid that whole scene in there, and here I am, and—I'm Orion—your destiny according to the saying." He offered a paint-speckled hand, which I didn't take.*

*"Fair enough," he said after a second. "I thought it was a pretty good line, but I guess not."*

*I let myself smile. "It's only bad if you pair it with a cheesy fake name."*

*"Ouch," he said, bringing a hand to his chest. "I don't have a choice about that part."*

*"Your name is really Orion? Like the constellation?"*

*"It's what people call me."*

*"Wow."*

*"I know."*

*"So were your parents hippies, or astronomers?"*

*"Maybe a little of both," he said.*

*"Well, it suits you, the name."*

*"Really? How's that?"*

"Orion was known for being extremely overconfident. Wasn't he?"

He smiled like he was impressed. "So the ice princess has a little fire to her. I like that."

"What does that mean—'ice princess'?"

"Isn't that who you are? Future wife to the heir of the empire?" He brushed a hand across the sky at the silhouette of the mountain, where the ski runs cut wide white paths through the dark of the trees.

I didn't know what to say to that. Or how this guy, who I'd never met, knew me as Shane's girlfriend. Or why it made something in me tense up that he did.

"I'm Julianna," I said finally. "And as far as I know, my future's not set in stone."

"Well—Julianna." He took a step toward me. In that moment his eyes danced with something I've gone back to more times than I can count, because of what he said next. "Maybe the saying is true then. Maybe we were supposed to meet out here on this balcony tonight."

I don't know why I wrote all of this down. . . .

Actually, that's a lie. I just lied in my own journal.

*I wrote it down because it's three a.m. and it's all I've thought about since I left Shane's. I wrote it down to remember it, because this night turned out to be beautiful.*

*We stayed out there under the stars, trading words like secrets, and I wanted to keep all of his for later. We talked about little things, like how he'd come here and stayed with his uncle for the winter because he wanted to try out a place different from the one he'd been in all his life. I said I wished I could go away too, but to a place tropical and warm, anywhere near an ocean. We talked about small towns and big dreams, about art and beauty and inspiration, and about traveling, and all the places we'd each want to see if we could. We talked like we'd always known each other, and when it finally came time for him to go, it felt like we had.*

*And I left too, because I didn't want to spend the night in Shane's bed after that. I wanted to come home and be alone, to think about it more. To think about him more. I hope that's not wrong. It doesn't seem like it should be, just talking to someone. What does seem wrong though, is that I've been lying in bed looking up at the real Orion in the sky, wondering if the one I met on the balcony had someone waiting on him, like Shane with me. I didn't ask, because if the answer was yes, I didn't want to know. It's almost enough to make me hope I never see him again. Almost.*

I close the journal but leave my finger in the space where she left off. All of a sudden this story feels different in a way I don't expect, and I'm not sure I want that. Shane and Julianna were the golden couple. That's how everyone remembers them. That's how I want to keep remembering them. But I can hear a tiny shift in her words. And I can see her standing on the balcony with Orion, the night shining around them with something new and magical. I've never been there personally, but I know enough to know that things like this never end well. Part of me hopes she didn't ever see him again, and part of me has a nervous feeling that maybe she did. I open the journal again to find out.

*May 26*

............

*I'm restless today and this town feels so small. Shane's gone, again. He's off learning to fly his grandpa's plane, and I'm here, waiting for him to get back, feeling pathetic. Days like these make me realize how much of my life revolves around him, and how little I have that's just me, or mine alone. Sitting here without him makes me feel totally unmoored—not in a free kind of way, but in a lonely one. The worst thing is, Shane's never made me feel like I had to give anything up for him. I did that all on my own, from the very beginning, almost without realizing.*

*But days like these, I realize a lot of things.*

*I don't have any close friends of my own. No best friend who knows everything about me, a person to call when I need someone besides Shane. After we got together his friends and the girls they dated became my friends, more out of circumstance than anything else. I like them, and I know them now, but I don't know if we'd be friends without him. It's like that with so many things. Shane's the reason for the music I listen to, the places I go, even the clothes I wear. They're all, in a way, because of him. Because I love him and, for me, that's always meant loving the things that make up his life. Some people might say that's how it should be, and others might say it's wrong. For me it's just the truth.*

*But when Mr. Kinney put that question on the board and gave us these books to answer it, it scared me. Made me think about the things I've done in my life so far. My one life. And aside from falling in love with Shane, I'm not sure I've done anything wild or precious, which makes me think about the future. We've talked about it. Made plans. He'll go to work for his family as soon as we graduate, and so will I. While he learns everything about running the mountain from his dad and grandfather, I'll work for one of his aunts—in one of the stores, or in the lodge, or the daycare—something important but not so important that I won't be able to quit when we get married and have kids, because in the Cruz household, there's nothing more important than family.*

*It's a future that would be perfect in so many ways, for so many reasons. But lately, if I let myself, I start to wonder if it'd be perfect for me. I keep going back to that quote, and to that night I spent talking with Orion, who was so different and free, he made me feel like I could be too. Like maybe I could do something that is mine alone.*

*I would paint, that's what I would do if I could choose anything.*

*I used to, a long time ago, before I came here. I used to love the barely-there weight of a brush in my hand, and the feeling that somewhere inside, I knew how to create something beautiful from nothing but a blank canvas and instinct. Aside from being with Shane, that feeling made me happier than anything else ever has. Like maybe it's who I really am, or what I'm really supposed to do. Which is why I've never told anyone, not even him. It feels too precious almost, to say it aloud. Like it would somehow take the magic away.*

*Shane would probably think it was cute if I ever told him. Anyone else would nod and smile at it like you do with a little girl who says she wants to be a singer or a model. But Mr. Kinney said to be idealistic here, so there it is. My big secret, on paper for all eternity. Maybe someday I'll be brave enough to actually do something about it. I can talk and write and daydream all I want about going places and making art and living a beautiful life, but if I never leave this town, if I just settle into what's easy and already there, I don't know if any of it will ever happen. I may read this ten years from now and it'll just make me sad.*

*I don't know why I'm like this today. Restless is the perfect word for it. I need to get out. Maybe I'll buy a new sketchbook and get in my car and just drive until I find someplace beautiful and inspiring. Maybe I'll do that, and in a way, it'll be like I'm flying too.*

I leave off for a second to reframe the image of Julianna in my mind, because reading this journal is a little like how I imagine it would be watching film develop. Not evenly or all at once, but in fragments and layers. I had no idea that Julianna Farnetti painted, or that the life she and Shane would've had together made her feel restless, or unsure. Why would I?

But I can see it now, and understand it. We all have something we hold close or dream about, something that maybe seems too dear to tell anyone. I have, ever since my dad published his book when I was little. I decided at eight that I wanted to write stories and poems like him. I did, too, in notebook after notebook. And I brought them all to him, and when he'd set everything aside to read my words, I felt that thing she talked about. That pure feeling of happiness at having created something from my own imagination. But then writing became a thing associated with my dad, which meant it was a thing my mother didn't like anymore. So I stopped. Probably for the same reasons Julianna stopped painting. It didn't fit into the life she had with a person she loved. I wouldn't have guessed it, but I understand this part of Julianna.

There's something else I think I understand reading her words, even though *she* probably didn't when she was writing them. Or maybe she did, but she couldn't bring herself to write it. But as a perfect stranger reading her words ten years later, I can see clear as day that her restlessness started to grow the night she met Orion.

## 12.

"We make ourselves a place apart,
Behind light words that tease and flout"
—"*REVELATION,*" *1915*

"I need a favor," I say. And it surprises me how bold it comes out sounding.

Trevor drops his hand from the dial on his locker and turns around to face me. "Says the girl I pulled out of the mud yesterday. Good morning to you, too." There's a smile in his voice, but he's surprisingly good at keeping a straight face.

"Sorry, I'm just in a hurry." I back up a step. "Good morning," I say, meeting his eyes. "Um . . . any chance you still have the keys to the art supply closet?"

With this I have his instant undivided attention, and it

takes everything in me not to hide behind my locker door like I usually do.

He steps toward me with a smile. "Maybe. Why?"

*Because I need a place to hide out and read Julianna's journal this period.* "Because I might wanna see it today . . ." I try to channel Kat and sound playful and sexy when I say it, but I'm no good, so I opt for a practical approach instead. "And because I want to go through the old student work and see if any of it belongs to the same kids who wrote the journals I'm working on for Kinney. I thought it'd be cool to send that to them too." *That sounds believable. I think.*

He just looks at me for a second, probably trying to make up his mind whether I'm lying or just lame. I'm not sure which one he settles on, but he seems genuine when he asks, "You need some help?"

"No, no, no," I say, trying to sound casual, only it comes out sounding ridiculous instead. "I'd rather be alone. Or, I mean, no. I don't need help. I just . . . it's a one-person job."

"Hm," he nods. "Too bad. I thought maybe you finally realized what you've been missing out on all these years." He digs around in his backpack, fishes out the lanyard, and hands it to me. "Here. Have fun. By yourself." Our fingers brush, just barely, when I take the keys, and I feel a little rush of gratitude and something else I decide to ignore. "Thanks," I say. "And thanks for yesterday too. I owe you."

"Don't worry about it." The bell rings and people slog by us, making their way to class, but we stay standing right there. Trevor clears his throat. "So did you want me to show you where it is or something?"

"Oh—I . . ." I flash back to my art supply closet daydream and feel my cheeks flush. "That's okay. I think I can find it myself. Down the hall from Kinney's room, right?"

"Yep."

"Perfect." I pick up the box of journals and turn to go. "Thanks again."

Trevor nods and we go our separate ways, and by the time I make it down the hall I feel a tiny pinprick of regret that I didn't just pretend I needed help finding it and let him walk me. Although that probably would've led to more awkwardness when it came time to open the door and slip inside. I would've had to turn him away at that point. I really do need the closet to myself.

I try and look casual as I wait next to the locked door for the second bell to ring. When I'm sure the hallway is empty, I slide the key in the doorknob, slip into the dark, and close the door quietly behind me. My hand finds the light switch on the wall, and when I flip it, I see I'm in a tiny room that's not all that different from what I imagined, except I'm alone and not kissing Trevor.

The shelves are a mess of cardboard boxes, some closed and some overflowing with paint-splotched brushes and palettes. Easels lean precariously in the corner; a fine, colored dust coats the floor. I decide there's no way Trevor actually brings any girls in here. It's not exactly romantic. Or even acceptably clean. But it is exactly what I'm looking for since I have to be at school but can't afford to be seen reading one of the journals I'm supposed to be sending out. Which I fully intend to finish doing once I read the rest of Julianna's.

I'm hooked now. I have to know what happens with Shane. Or Orion. I grab a stiff tarp from one of the shelves and sit down.

## June 2

.........

*I went looking for inspiration today and I found Orion. Sitting on the beach of the little lake I think of as my secret. I still can't believe he was there. Since the night we met I keep catching myself thinking of him when I shouldn't be. Wondering where he is when I have no reason to care. When I left the party that night, we didn't exchange numbers or talk about seeing each other again. That would've crossed the line I'd already tiptoed up to by letting myself get so swept up by the sparkling cold of the night and the warm brown of his eyes. When I left Shane's house, I knew the only way I might ever see Orion again was by chance.*

*I can't say I wasn't hoping for it, but I didn't see it coming.*

*The only thing I saw was the twisty, narrow trail in front of me and the green of the pine trees lining it all the way up to the lake. I used to take this same trail when I wanted to be by myself, and I'd lie there in the sun on the white pumice beach and listen to the wind whisper like far off rushing water through the tops of the trees. There's something special about it up there, away from everything and everyone.*

McCloud is a lake like a secret, tucked deep in a little valley between tall gray mountains. The water is this deep blue-green that's so still and clear you can see the reflections of the clouds drifting by on the surface, and the dark outlines of fallen trees suspended beneath it. It's like a dream place, where two worlds meet. At least it was today.

At the top of the hill where the trail opens up to the beach and the lake, I stopped short when I saw someone else was there. When I saw Orion was there. He was sitting cross-legged on a log near the edge of the water, bent over a sketch pad in his lap, pencil moving in short, quick strokes, no idea that he wasn't alone. I froze.

I knew I should leave before he saw me. That I probably shouldn't be here, alone with him. But I wanted him to look up. Meet my eyes. And smile like he remembered every detail of that first night the way I did. I watched a moment too long before deciding I should turn around, but by then it was too late. That was all it took.

He glanced up, and a smile hovered at the corners of his mouth, but he didn't seem surprised to see me there. "Hi," he said.

It was so casual the way he said it, and he was so out of place I had to laugh. "Hi?"

"Yeah. That's typically what I say to people I know when
I see them. Don't you?"

"Who says you know me?"

"Who says I don't?" He set his pencil down and smiled.
It was quiet a moment. "So either you're following me or I
was right about the whole fate thing."

"Or maybe this is just a small town, where people run
into each other all the time."

"At deserted lakes?" He looked around to make his point.

"I promise I wasn't following you. You somehow found
your way to the one spot I didn't think I would see anyone."

"Coincidence, then."

The word lingered between us, and I thought of how
many times I'd hoped for a coincidence like this since the
night we met. "What are you doing here, anyway?"

He held up the pad in explanation, then set it on the log.
"Drawing. Enjoying the day. Thinking of going for a
swim. You?"

"I just . . . wanted to get out for a little while, and so I
came here and . . ." And there he was, and the sight of him

*sitting there was almost enough to make me believe maybe there was a reason. He smiled again, and the warm brown of his eyes tempted me to sit down next to him and forget everything else. I looked at the ground. "I should go," I said, but I didn't mean it.*

*"I can leave if you want." He stood, but he didn't mean it either.*

*"No, you were here first. You should . . ." I paused, unsure of what I wanted to say. "You should stay."*

*"Then you should too." His eyes tried to catch mine, but I looked away again at the water, the mountains, the sky. Anywhere but at him, because I was afraid of what he might be able to see. Because all of a sudden it didn't feel like we were standing on the beach anymore. It felt like we were balanced on a thin, thin line. That fragile one that divides the invisible space between something and nothing, or before and after.*

I stop there to reread the last sentence, and I know exactly what she means. And I can see it's really happening. She's really falling for him, and he is for her, and on the one hand I know it's wrong, because she has Shane and they love each other and they're perfect for each other. But the way she writes it, I think I might've fallen for Orion too.

If I were her, I maybe even would have thought it was

meant to be somehow. Despite the fact that it was wrong. Whatever it is there between them seems like the kind of thing that happens in life only if you're lucky. But she might have actually had it with him. That connection or pull that's there is sweet and romantic, and the sap in me wants to soak it up and see where it goes. I check my phone and flip a few pages to see how much more of this entry there is. I probably have just enough time to finish it.

*We didn't cross that line today. He sat, picked up his notebook, and went back to sketching. I found a place close, but not too close, on the grainy white beach to sit and take off my shoes so I could dip my toes in the icy water. I lay back on my elbows and watched the sun sparkle on the surface of it. Let the warmth and the quiet soak in. And for a while we balanced there on the line like that, not saying anything, though more than once I thought I felt his eyes on me.*

*"What are you drawing?" I asked him.*

*"The trees." He pointed with his pencil at a group close to where we were sitting. They were more like skeletons of trees, with bare branches and no sign of life left on them. On one of them someone had carved the words* I WAS HERE *into the bark, which seemed eerie and sad in a way.*

*"Can I see?"*

*He slid off the log onto the ground next to me and handed me his sketchbook. The trees on the page didn't look like the real ones at all. They danced with shadow and light and practically swayed in the breeze that blew cool and soft over us. Even the words I WAS HERE looked freshly carved into the bark.*

*"This is beautiful." I traced my finger over the branches.*

*He looked down, seeming almost embarrassed or shy about it. "Thanks."*

*"No, really. This is like something you'd see in a gallery. It's . . . is art something you want to do for a living?" The thought of it, of him, wanting the same thing I did ran electric through me.*

*He shook his head and took the pad back. "Not really. I've thought about it, but for now I just kind of do it for myself."*

*I nodded, so close to telling him I felt the same way about painting. That I understood, or used to. That a long time ago I knew what it was like to do something purely for myself. But then I noticed the black ink of a tattoo on the underside of his forearm. I wanted to reach out and touch it, but I pointed instead. "So is that just for yourself too, or can I see what it is?"*

*He looked down and turned his wrist so I could see it. "That . . . was my sixteenth birthday present from my brother. It's what he does." He glanced from the tattoo to me. "I thought it was cool three years ago, but it's kinda cheesy now, huh?"*

*"That depends on if you just picked a symbol off the wall or if you got it because it actually means something to you." I looked again at the three joined spirals, then brought my eyes back to his. "Does it? Mean anything?"*

*"If I tell you, you can't laugh. Like I said, I was sixteen. And I thought I was being deep."*

*"I promise," I said, ready to laugh. Then without thinking I ran my fingers over it just like I'd done with his drawing.*

*His arm tensed under my touch. I drew my hand back. He cleared his throat. I looked at my lap. And the moment hung there between us, heavy, like clouds before a storm.*

*"It's called a triskelion," he said. "Each spiral stands for something." He pointed to the top one. "There's motion, like taking action or moving forward. There's evolution— that's growing or changing with life. And then there's illumination, which is understanding or knowing." He paused, maybe waiting for me to laugh, but I didn't.*

"It's like the three parts of life," I said.

"Yeah. The parts I want to remember to do." He smiled, then picked up a piece of pumice and tossed it in the water, where it floated on the glassy surface in front of us. "You ever go swimming in this lake?"

"Never." I wiggled my toes and felt the icy needles of the water.

"You want to?"

I shook my head.

"I think I might." He stood up and pulled his shirt over his head, then went for the belt that hung low on his hips.

I forced my eyes away from his bare chest and out to the center of the water, hoping it might temper the tingly warmth that spread out in my own chest, knocking my heart around against my ribs. "I think I'll wait here," I said. "With my clothes on."

He stepped out of his jeans and tossed them over the log. "Suit yourself." Then without another look at me he turned, took two long strides toward the water, and dove into the icy blue of the lake. Just like that. Fearless. When he came up, he was gasping for air. "Holy shit, that's cold!" He half laughed, and made his way back to me at the edge of the water, where he waded back out onto the beach.

"Damn, that was colder than I expected."

"It's melted snow." I pointed to the white patches still tucked into the shady crags of the mountains above us. "You probably just shocked your whole nervous system."

"Maybe." He shrugged, then shivered. "Sometimes a shock to the system is a good thing, you know? Like a reminder that you're alive." He sat on the log next to me, dripping ice cold water, bare skin covered with goose bumps, and the biggest smile on his face.

I looked out at the surface of the lake where the sunlight broke into tiny diamonds and spread out sparkling across it. "And that you have one wild and precious life."

He turned to me, and we were so close I could almost smell the sun and the lake on his skin. "That's deep of you."

"You should talk." I shoved him off the log, hoping he didn't notice the sudden embarrassment in my voice. "It's from a poem I read in English."

"And what's the rest say?"

*"I don't know the rest. Just the one line I liked. 'Tell me, what is it you plan to do with your one wild and precious life.'"*

*"So." He smiled through chattering teeth. "What do you plan to do with yours, Julianna Farnetti?"*

*"In a perfect world?"*

*"Yeah. If you could do anything you wanted. Without worrying about what people expect of you or have planned out or anything else. What would you do with your life?" His eyes rested on mine, waiting, and it made me feel vulnerable in a way, like maybe he knew about feeling restless or understood about wanting something more. Somewhere in the trees behind us, a twig snapped. A tiny ripple splashed against the shore. And the wall I'd spent so many years building crumbled.*

*"I'd make art," I said. "Paintings, that would make people feel something when they looked at them." I paused, surprised at how easy it was to tell him what I always keep so close around everyone else. And then the rest came tumbling out before I could stop it. "And I'd leave here and travel, like we talked about. I'd watch the sun rise over different mountains and set into crystal oceans. And—" I caught myself before I could say the next thing I'd thought of. That I would have met him sooner. Or in a different situation, when there could have been a chance for something.*

"And what?" he asked.

"And . . . I'd have no regrets," I answered. "Which is
why I need to do this." I gave the water one more glance
and made up my mind.

Then before I could change it, I stood, peeled off my tank
top and shorts, and took a running start. The second
my fingertips touched the surface, sparks of ice lit my
body up and stole my breath away, but I forced myself
to go under. To feel the electricity there before I came up,
laughing and gasping for air.

And when I broke through the surface, I could almost
swear I came up as someone new.

Orion jumped in again with me, and we swam for as
long as we could stand the cold, legs brushing and hearts
pounding and teeth chattering.

I've always thought I'm most myself when I'm with
Shane, but today with Orion I was most like who I want
to be. I was someone different and bold and honest. Not
embarrassed or unsure about anything. Not even the feel
of his eyes taking in the lines of my body, or the quiet
shush of pencil moving over paper as he drew me there on
the beach, drying in the afternoon sun.

I stop at the doodle at the bottom of the page. Orion's tattoo. She went home and drew it in her journal, like a memento from the day. I'm about to go back and reread what he said it meant when the high-pitched monotone of the bell rings out above my head. I jump at the sound of it, and it takes me a good few seconds to get my bearings and go from watching Julianna and Orion fall for each other at the edge of McCloud Lake to gathering up my stuff so I can make it to second period.

I tuck Julianna's journal in my backpack, grab the box full of the others I still haven't finished addressing, and ease open the closet door, wondering if I'm the only person in the world besides the two of them who knows about this. I wonder where it went from there. If they saw each other again. Where Orion ended up. If Shane ever found out. What he would've done. The leap my mind makes at that last thought is a dark one and I dismiss it quickly before I slip out the door.

In the hallway it's crowded and bright and feels worlds away from Julianna and the story that's unfolding on the pages of her journal. It's all I can do not to duck back in the closet and finish reading. As much as I want to, though, I can't miss a second day of all my classes for that. But nothing says I can't pick it back up after school. Maybe even up at the lake where chance brought them together and choice made them stay.

## 13.

"Some say the world will end in fire,
Some say ice.
From what I've tasted of desire
I hold with those who favor fire."
—"FIRE AND ICE," 1920

The dead trees are how I know I'm in the right place. Only now it's not just a few at the edge of the lake. All of the trees around McCloud are dead from the volcanic gas that started leaking up through the ground years ago. It had probably just started when Julianna and Orion were up there. For a while the whole area was closed down, but then the scientists, or forest service, or whoever decides those things, determined it was safe for people to be in the area, even though the trees were dying. I never came up here after that, and the utterly deserted feeling it has makes me think not many other people do either.

When I get out of the car, it's so quiet in the parking lot I can almost hear my own heartbeat. The bleached white skeletons of the trees stand stiff against the gray afternoon sky like ghosts, which seems appropriate. It's creepy enough to make me question what I'm doing here alone. I could just as easily hole myself up in my room to read the rest of the journal. But like yesterday, something in me wants to see the place Julianna wrote about—where she once swam in a sparkling lake, lay under the midday sun, and fell for a boy she wasn't supposed to.

But it's so different here from how she wrote it, and it makes me a little sad as I look around at the emptiness. It's dead. A shadow of what it used to be. I wanted to see this place the way she did—beautiful and dreamy, and romantic. I thought maybe there would be something of that left. Some little piece of her world that's been here all this time, like another secret I might be let in on. But there's no life or beauty or magic up here. There's only whitewashed trees and a sky that's getting darker by the minute.

I came to see the lake, so I grab her journal and a sweatshirt just in case the clouds in the distance move in, and I head across the parking lot. The sign at the trailhead says it's a mile up to the lake, but as I step onto the trail, I remember her journal entry and feel like I'm closer than that. Like I'm right there with her, climbing the steep hill, maybe to end up at something I didn't see coming. The trail is narrow and twisty like she said, and between the gnarled roots pushing up through the dirt and the loose rocks all around, I have to keep my eyes on the ground directly in front of me to keep from tripping.

As I walk, a sound like a soft, continuous exhale moves through the trees high above me, and I pause for a moment, startled and unsure of what it is. But then I feel the stray wisps of the breeze that made it; they reach down through the branches, lifting a few strands of my hair, making them dance around me. And I remember what she called this place. A dream world, she'd said, where two worlds meet. She'd been talking about herself and Orion. Today, it feels like her world and mine. It seems perfectly fitting that I should read her journal in this spot. There's something poetic about it. But more than once on the way up, I have to convince myself that Julianna didn't somehow, from beyond, put her journal in my hands for me to find, that the place is not haunted, and that I am not crazy for coming up here to do this.

After what seems like farther than a mile, the trail opens up to a rocky white beach, where the lapping of the water on the shore is the only sound besides the constant shush of the breeze. That part is just like she said. And the lake. Tucked down against sheer gray rock on the back side, it still sits perfectly calm and blue. Even in the pale afternoon light I can see straight through to the bottom, where so many dead trees have fallen in it looks like a forest has grown beneath the surface. I turn around to look for a decent place to sit, and that's when I see the letters carved into a tree, just a few feet from where I stand.

I WAS HERE.

Chills shoot down my back and out through my feet. In that instant it feels like she's talking to me, telling me I'm in the right place. It has to be the carving she mentioned in the journal, that Orion drew before he drew her. Which means she really was here. *They* were here together. So close. Maybe in this exact spot. It does feel like knowing a secret, and I sit down right there to read.

*June 3*
.........

*Shane gave me a gift today and I could barely look him in the eye. We sat in his Jeep at the edge of the creek, and when I opened the box from the jeweler, and it sparkled in the sun, I should have felt happy. I should've felt lucky that he's so sweet and giving and the one person who knows me best of anyone. But the only thing I felt was something heavy that started to twist, deep and tight, in my chest.*

*"It's beautiful," I said.*

*And it was, but it wasn't anything I would've chosen for myself. Inside the box, on a layer of white satin, was a lacy silver snowflake, intricate and inlaid with tiny diamonds over the entire thing. The perfect necklace for his ice princess. He took it out when I didn't and held it up so it spun in the sunlight at the end of its delicate chain.*

"I thought it looked like you. Here." He undid the clasp and I automatically swept my hair to the side so he could hook it at the back of my neck.

"It's perfect," he said. And he sat back and smiled, and the thing in my chest twisted even tighter, and the front seat of his Jeep felt ten times smaller, because at that moment the only thing I could think about was Orion. And of how much more I'd felt like me at the lake with him yesterday than I did in Shane's car right then.

I brought my hand to where the necklace hung on my chest, felt the new weight of it around my neck. "It really is beautiful, but you didn't need to do this. . . . I don't . . ."

I searched his face, nervous all of a sudden about what he might be able to see written on mine. It seems ridiculous, but I was worried he'd look at me and know something was off. Maybe even be able to see that since the day at the lake, I haven't stopped thinking about Orion, and it's made a mess of me. Nothing happened between us. Nothing physical, anyway. We never touched, and after a while, we hardly even spoke. But I felt different. Torn. And today I was afraid Shane would notice. It made me want to hide.

"Why did you do this?" I asked him. It was heavy, the guilt of feeling what I did, and it came out more as an accusation than a question.

"Wow. Do I need a reason? I just wanted to surprise you." He leaned back against the seat and looked out his window, and I could feel the distance between us stretch beyond the space between our two seats. "If you don't like it you can take it back," he said after a moment. I didn't answer. "Am I missing something? Because you're acting weird."

I put a hand on his leg, wanting to smooth the tension away. "No, no. I'm sorry. I didn't mean to sound that way. I love it. I just wasn't expecting this . . ."

"That's usually how surprises work," he said, a smile returning.

I leaned over the seat and took his face in my hands, kissed him on both cheeks. "It's perfect, thank you. You're too good to me. You know that, right?" My stomach clenched when I said it, because of how true it was.

"I could never be too good to you, Jules." He smiled again and ran his fingers through my hair, and then, through lips that kissed mine, he whispered, "I love you."

"I love you, too," I told him. And I meant it. But today when I said it, the words felt distant.

I shiver again. I know the necklace she's talking about. They found it on the river's edge, not far from Shane's Jeep.

June 6
·········

*I've been thinking about the picture Orion drew of me at the lake. He closed his sketchbook without showing me, so I didn't ask. We walked down the trail together, quiet, and when we got to my car, he smiled and gave me a tiny slip of paper. A fortune. I laughed when I looked down and read the words he said to me the first night we met, about meeting your destiny while trying to avoid it. And then I went quiet when I turned it over and saw a phone number on the back. A moment went by where we didn't say anything, like we both knew what it could mean if I took it.*

*"If you ever need to find me," he said.*

*I nodded and put it in my pocket, and we went our separate ways.*

*I haven't seen him since, but there isn't anything I want to do more. I don't know how I can feel this way about someone who's so different from Shane, or who, really, I hardly know. But it doesn't feel like that with him. Orion feels like someone I've always known, but also someone I need to know more.*

*I got in my car yesterday and drove circles around town, then up to the lakes hoping the entire time to find him by accident again, without having to cross that line and call him. And the whole time I was pleading with fate, or chance, or whatever, for him to find me. Just find me again. Find me and take me somewhere secret, where I can be who I am when I'm with him. I even told myself that if we did somehow find each other, it would mean something. Maybe something important enough to justify the way I feel.*

*But he wasn't anywhere.*

*I came home and stared at the numbers etched out in pencil for a long, long time. Read the fortune over and over. Thought about what I would say to Orion if he picked up. Calling him, period, would say it all: that I needed to find him.*

*I didn't. Thank God I didn't. I tucked the slip of paper away in the back of this book, safe like all of the other secrets I've put down in here. And now I'm going to close it up tight. Pack it away. This is dangerous, what I'm doing.*

*Shane's supposed to call soon to go out tonight, and that's where my head and my heart should both be. With him.*

I stop reading, positive now that I know where this is going. Then I turn the page. The entry is short, but I can tell from the very first line that I'm right.

June 7

.........

*A moment was all it took to change everything. A moment to sit alone in my room after Shane told me he was going out with his friends tonight. A moment to justify dialing Orion's number. To slip out my front door and into the warmth of his car waiting in my driveway. A moment to end up at the hot springs under a glittering sky and a fresh dusting of snow, to feel the fire of the water and the ice of the air mix between us. For hands to brush skin, and lips to meet beneath the moonless sky.*

*A moment for want to erase thought.*

*A moment for him to pull back and search my eyes for a reason to stop.*

*A moment for me to close them against every last one and press my lips to his.*

*A moment was all it took to lose my balance on this tightrope I've been walking.*

*And now I don't know what comes after this.*

*I don't know what comes next.*

I drop the journal in my lap. Oh my God, Julianna. I know what comes next.

In two days you and Shane will graduate. You'll pose for a picture in your gowns, with your hats crooked on your heads and your arms around each other. That night a storm will blow in out of nowhere. The two of you will go to a party, then leave together, and that will be the last anyone ever sees of you. Some will say Shane was drunk. Others will say you both were. A few people will think they remember you having a fight.

The next morning a snowplow will spot Shane's Jeep half buried at the bottom of the ravine before you're even reported missing. Search and rescue will be called out when it's found empty. Half the town will volunteer to help, including my dad and uncle. They won't find you, but they will find some of your things—Shane's leather wallet, with everything still in it. A tiny diamond snowflake. Two graduation tassels. And blood in the snow.

Then, after a week of searches and vigils and prayers, it'll be announced that you and Shane were swept down the river into Summit Lake. That a further search will have to wait for the summer when the ice on the lake melts completely, but even then, the chances of recovering anything are slim. The lake is deep, and below the surface it narrows like the neck of an hourglass before opening up into an underground cavern. Few of those lost in it are ever found.

People will cover the shore with flowers that stand out bright against the melting patches of snow. They'll leave prayer candles, whose glass will crack from the cold, spilling out wax of different colors. The whole town will come to the memorial at the edge of the half-frozen lake. A little girl will watch the grief hang heavy on the people's faces, not understanding or really knowing what was lost.

Until ten years later.

It's unsettling to think that this is what happened two days before. Two days before they left a party together and ended up dead. From a car crash. In his Jeep. Where maybe they had a fight. It could have just been the icy road and the blinding snow that caused it. But what if that wasn't it at all? What if she told Shane about Orion, or he found out some other way? Maybe anger or hurt or shock was what sent them hurtling over the edge. And all this time they've been remembered as something that wasn't true at all: Lakes High's golden couple. A legacy unknowingly built on a lie.

I don't know what to think. The second I start to judge her for what she did, I feel bad. She was seventeen. Torn. Felt something for Orion that was enough to make her question what she had with Shane. But it's unnerving to find out something isn't actually like you always imagined it. To see the tarnish just past the shine, or find a crack in the glossy finish. And there's something else. The sketch that she wrote about sounds eerily similar to one I've seen hanging behind the counter at Kismet. It's one I've noticed before when I ordered, but never *really* looked at.

A fat raindrop plops onto the open page of Julianna's journal, smudging the ink, and then another and another. I shut it quickly and tuck it up under my shirt, then make a run for the trail down. Miraculously, I make it to my car just before the sky opens up. I sit in the seat for a moment, catching my breath and watching the rain pound the windshield. Julianna's journal rests on the dash, damp but safe. There are two more entries before her story ends and the pages go blank. I don't want to get there just yet, so instead I turn the key and I drive. I need to see that sketch up close.

14.

"But oh, the agitated heart
Till someone really find us out."
—*"REVELATION," 1915*

Inside Kismet it's warm and cozy, and surprisingly empty for
a rainy day. The bells on the door jangle when I step in, but
no one's behind the counter, which is actually perfect. I spent
the entire drive down from the lakes trying to figure out how
I could get a closer look at the sketches hanging on the wall
behind the register. Whereas all of the art on the walls of
Kismet is in constant flux, these three have never moved.
They've always been there, for as long as I remember, right
in front of me.

I know it's a crazy thought, but I have to see if one of
them could possibly be the one of Julianna that Orion drew

that day at the lake. Because if it is, that means . . . I don't know exactly, but it feels like something. Maybe that Josh knew Orion? Was friends with him? Or maybe he's his brother. Ex-tattoo-artist-turned-coffee-shop-owner? That would explain the full sleeves on both arms. I realize as I think each of these things how crazy they'd sound if I said them out loud, but at the moment I don't care about the lack of logic in it. For now I hope that maybe the feeling is enough to lead me to something.

I stand in the middle of the empty café a moment, waiting for someone to appear from the back room, and hoping it's Lane. He's not intimidating to me in the same way Josh is, so I could actually carry on a conversation with him. Maybe even ask him if he knows anything about the sketches. No one comes out, but I can hear a steady rhythm from the back room that sounds like something heavy being moved and then stacked. Whoever it is working back there probably didn't hear me come in, which means I might have a minute or two to inspect the sketches before they even realize I'm here.

I inch my way toward the register and the three frames behind it. After one look over my shoulder, and another at the door of the storeroom, I step through the opening in the counter, past the register and stacks of paper coffee cups, and come face to face with three framed sketches, the middle of which is the "sexy girl," as Kat calls her.

The picture is of her in profile, and she's lying on her back on what I always pictured as a beach rather than the shore of a lake. She's stretched out on her back, one knee bent so her leg forms a triangle, chin tilted toward the sky, eyes closed, hair tumbling down over her shoulders. She's smiling, just barely, like maybe she's dreaming. Or soaking up the sun after a swim. Nothing about it jumps out at me as distinctly Julianna, but there isn't anything that says it couldn't be her either. From what I know, a sketch is an imprecise art form.

I look at the two on either side, the ones I never paid much attention to before today. They're of trees. Not dying trees, but trees with branches that wave like arms on the page so that I can practically see the wind in them. I lean in closer, sure I'm going to see I WAS HERE carved into one of them, and—

"What can I do for you?"

The voice makes me jump—no, leap—backward. "Oh, God," I say, hand to my chest. My heart pounds so hard against it, I think Josh must be able to hear it too. "I'm so sorry," I add. "I just . . . I just was trying to get a closer look at these drawings." I point, as if that will somehow explain everything and lessen the sudden burn in my cheeks.

Josh nods slowly but doesn't look at them or say anything and I feel like I've been caught trying to steal something.

"They're beautiful," I say, watching him closely—for what, I'm not sure. There's a hint of something I can't pin.

He tries for a smile but it just looks tired. And he doesn't even look at the drawings. "Thanks." There's a pause, and then, "Did you want to order something?"

"Yeah, I—wait." His *thanks* echoes inside my head. "Are they *yours*?" I ask. "Did you draw those?"

"Yeah." His eyebrows crash together for a second like he's surprised at his own answer. "Long time ago." We're quiet a moment, and then he recovers, focusing on me. "So can I get you something to drink? You look like you have some work to do." He nods at Julianna's journal, which I realize is clutched tight to my chest.

"This? No, it's not work, it's—" I stop myself and take a deep breath, but a host of questions and suspicions are whirling in my head, fighting to come out of mouth. "Yeah, I'll take a . . .um . . ."

"You want a chai, like normal?"

"Yes. Please." I force my mouth shut and try to look at the ground, collect myself. But as soon as he turns to grab a mug, my eyes creep back up to the girl on the wall.

"Who is she?" I blurt out. A lot less tactfully than I'd like to.

He turns with the pitcher of tea in his hand and looks at me like he either doesn't know what I mean or doesn't want to answer.

"The girl in the drawing," I stammer. "Did you know her?"

"I did." He says it in a way that makes it clear he isn't going to elaborate. And then he glances at the sketch, just barely, before going back to making my drink, and I see it. A flicker of something. *Such a tiny thing, a glance,* Julianna wrote. And his glance says something.

Before I can form a response, the door opens, letting in a whoosh of cool air, and Trevor Collins steps in, shaking the rain from his hair. A smile breaks across his face when he sees me. "Hey, Frost. I thought that was your car outside."

"Hi," I manage. My mind is spinning a million miles a second with what I think I just saw. With what really has been right here in front of me this whole time. I'm so close to *something*, I know it. The last thing I need is to complicate it with Trevor Collins, cute as he looks with his hair all damp, and his eyes a vibrant blue against the gray outside. What I need is to keep talking to Josh. Ask him some more questions to be sure.

Trevor looks around at the empty café. "You alone? Where's your partner in crime?"

"I don't know," I say curtly. "Either sick or ditching. She wasn't at school today." I turn my back to him and dig out a few dollars to pay, hoping he's not planning on staying.

"Oh," he says from behind me. "I was gonna head up to the mountain for a few runs, but it's all gonna be slush now." There's a pause. "You want some company?"

The question zings straight to my stomach, makes my cheeks flame up. There's no joking or pretense to it. I can hear the smile in his voice when he asks, picture it without turning around, and any other day—well, lately at least, I might've actually said okay. But it feels like I'm right on the edge of discovering something that would change every-thing, and I need to get back there.

I turn around. "Not today." His smile takes a tumble, and the zing I felt turns into a stab of regret. I soften my tone a little. "I'm sorry—I just have a lot of work to do—my speech. Maybe another time?"

"Here you go," Josh says before Trevor can answer.

I turn back to the counter and hand him my three dollars, trying to figure out how I can pick our sort-of conversation back up after Trevor leaves. But when Josh reaches out to take my money, all the thoughts in my head grind to a screeching halt. I only catch a glimpse of it when I put the money in his palm, but it's enough to recognize it. On his forearm, buried in a maze of other tattoos, is a tiny triple spiral.

I gasp. Audibly.

"You okay?" he asks. Josh, Orion, I don't know what to call him right now.

I nod wordlessly and he slides my cup across the counter to me. When I grab it and turn around, I almost run into Trevor. "Some other time then," he mumbles. He looks through me, at Josh. "I'll take a hot chocolate. To go."

I wish I could explain that I'm not blowing him off, because I can see on his face that's what he thinks is going on, and I feel awful about it, especially since this time he seemed sincere. Sincerely interested, even. But at the moment, the only thing my brain can do is try to reconcile the fact that Josh is Orion. Or Orion is Josh.

"See you tomorrow?" I ask, a cheery octave higher than normal.

"Sure," Trevor says, measurably aloof now. I don't blame him, but I don't try to stop him either. He turns without saying anything else, and I do too, and we go our separate ways. With my hands shaking I head to the table in the far corner, where I can pretend to bury myself in work while sorting out the fact that the Orion Julianna wrote about is standing right here in this café, with a different name, and seems to be a whole different person than when she knew him.

I open up her journal to where I left off and get a pen out of my purse like I'm going to write something down. Trevor pays for his hot chocolate and glances over at me one more time just before he pushes out the door. I smile briefly and drop my eyes to the page in front of me, but I don't read the words. I hardly even breathe. Trevor walks out the door and Josh busies himself with unloading the box of coffee bags, and I take a good long look at him from the safety of my corner.

For a second I think I can see him there. Orion. Not as he is now—barely thirty but already weighed down with life. But as he was with her. I can see him standing on the balcony under the stars, diving into the freezing lake, falling in love with a girl he could never have. I wonder what happened after. Who she chose before—

"Hey, I gotta go finish up in the back," he says, breaking down the empty box in his hands. "Just yell if you need a refill."

"Thanks," I answer. And I leave it at that for now. Before I can ask him anything else, I have to know how it ended. The pages of the journal are a little damp from the rain, but the ink hasn't smeared or bled. I take a deep breath, a sip of the too-hot chai, and brace myself for what comes next. For where the story ends.

## 15.

"I have been one acquainted with the night."
—*"ACQUAINTED WITH THE NIGHT," 1928*

### June 8

.........

*I woke up afraid today. Afraid of what I've done, of what it means, of what I feel, and of what I could lose because of it all. Shane has been my constant every day for the past four years of my life, and until now I thought he was my future, too. And it was safe, that thought, and known, and seemed like how it should be. I don't want to lose the comfort of his hand sliding into mine or the smile on his face when he talks about what that future together will look like. The thing I can't stand more than the thought of losing him is the thought of hurting him. I don't want* to know what his face will look like if I tell him what I've done. What I chose. I don't think I could look him in the eye. But I don't know if I have a choice in that anymore. I think I have to tell him that I stepped off the edge I've been balancing on since the night I met Orion. Because I don't think there's any coming back from that.

What I'm most afraid of, though, is that I don't know if I want to come back from it. I'm afraid of wanting to sink deeper into it. Shane is all of the things I thought I wanted. Orion is freedom and possibility, and so many other things that feel like what I need. When I close my eyes I can still feel the warmth of his mouth on mine, and the heat of the water, and the cold of the night, all wrapped around us like we belonged to it, and I don't want to let that go because it was the most intense thing I've ever felt.

But I couldn't look at him right now either, because that night when he brought me home, I lied. I told him it was a mistake, that it never should have happened, and that I didn't want to see him again.

"That's what you really want?" he asked. Hurt washed over his face, pooled in his eyes, and I knew he didn't believe me.

I closed mine a second so he wouldn't see me waver. When I opened them again, I looked at him in the dark, and I *said, "That's what I need. I need to not see you again." It was the last thing I said to him. And then I went into my house and I cried, because of the look on his face and the awful taste of my own words. It wasn't what I wanted or needed.*

*I tried to fix it today. I called his house, but it just rang and rang until finally his uncle picked up. He said Orion had packed his bags first thing in the morning, told him he was going home, and that he wasn't coming back. Maybe I should be relieved, but I only feel empty now.*

*Tomorrow I'll seal this journal up and turn it in to Mr. Kinney to pack away for ten years. The day after, I'll put on my graduation gown, walk down the aisle, and get my diploma. After that it's blank, like the rest of the pages in this book. Empty. I was supposed to answer the question about what it is I plan to do with my life, and it was supposed to be something beautiful and filled with hope. Something I could look back on ten years from now to be reminded not to give up on the things I want most in life. What I'm afraid of now is that I'll look back, and I'll see that's exactly what I've just done.*

I sit there stunned. Angry, almost. That *is* what she did. She let the wrong one go. She lied to him and to herself about how she felt, and he left before she had a chance to tell him any different. He left, and she died, and that really was the last thing she said to him. I wonder what the last thing she said to Shane was. For all I know they died in the middle of a fight.

I hate it. This can't be how it ends. When I took Julianna's journal, I thought it was going to be the real words of a girl who was more like a myth in my mind. And it has been. But I also thought it would be the perfect love story of the perfect couple that disappeared together, which, as far as endings go, is tragic. But there was even something romantic about that too—them perishing together, like Romeo and Juliet, or Tristan and Isolde. I sometimes used to imagine that none of those couples really died, because they were together. That somehow, leaving the world with one's true love allowed them a different kind of ending, where they lived on together in their own paradise, far from the real world that ended in tragedy. It was my way of making a happy ending, I guess. But there isn't one here. The story I've always known was based on a different perception altogether. One that never accounted for Orion.

He comes out from the back just then, and I watch him from behind the journal. There are so many things I want to say. To ask. Why he didn't fight for her. Didn't even argue when she told him to leave. Wouldn't he have? If he felt like she did? When did he come back to town, and why did he stay, even after she was gone?

Josh/Orion glances my way and I drop my eyes back to the journal. I'm scared to look at him because of what I know. I feel guilty for it. It's one thing to know the secrets of someone you'll never look in the eye. But it's an entirely different thing to know things about the person standing in front of you. Painful things, that he's probably tried to bury deep in work and art. Maybe that explains why he is the way he is—kind of distant, always with a hint of sadness to him, always alone. He's one of those people who seem only halfway there, always listening to some low, wistful song in the background of his mind.

Behind the counter Josh grabs a big round mug, pours tea and then milk in, and takes it over to the steamer. He does it automatically, like he's not thinking about it, so much as just going through the motions. I stop my deep character analysis when he turns with the mug on a saucer and heads my way. I pretend to be looking at a picture to my right. It's part of the patchwork of art covering the walls. The still lifes and abstracts, paintings and sketches, all form the constantly evolving backdrop in the café. I've watched so many of my favorites move around on the walls to make places for new art, which is what I think this one that I'm looking at is. I've never noticed it before.

*Clink.* Josh sets the chai on the table and I look up into warm brown eyes. "Thought that one might be cold by now." He nods at my full cup, and then his eyes flick to the journal, which is sitting facedown on the table. "Must be some absorbing work there."

"Thanks," I say, and look back at the painting because if I don't focus on something besides him, I won't be able to keep all of my questions to myself. And I need to think about all this before I say anything. *If* I say anything.

"That one's something, isn't it?" He's looking at the painting too.

I nod. Where so many sunset paintings look peaceful and calm, melancholy is woven into every brushstroke of this one. It's a twilight image of the familiar dark razor peak silhouettes of the Minarets, looking icy and stoic. The only warmth in the painting comes from a barely visible sliver of golden light behind the mountains. The last of the sun. Above that the sky pales, then deepens to violet, faintly lit by a delicate wash of stars and the tiny sliver of moon. It's a skyline I've fallen asleep looking at most nights of my life, but the feeling in it is so lonely and sad it's hard to believe it's the same one.

Josh tilts his head one way and then the other, looking at it from slightly different angles. "It's called *Acquainted with the Night.*"

"Like the Robert Frost poem," I say, still looking at the painting. At the stars. "That fits."

And it does. I can't take my eyes off it. Not only does it capture the feel of the poem perfectly, but it seems to embody Frost's whole view of nature, with its austere but beautiful indifference to us and our comparably tiny lives. The little control we actually have over them. "It's a sad poem," I say, glancing at Josh.

"Yeah? I don't know it. But it feels like that, doesn't it? Sad."

His question hangs in the air above us a moment, and I'm not sure what to say. I want to ask him who the artist is. My eyes search the canvas for the answer, but there's no signature that I can see. There is, however, something else. Something that takes my breath a second time, because I've already seen and recognized it once today. It's tiny—barely discernable if you didn't already know what it was: a set of three swirling spirals brushed into the dark silhouette of a mountain. It matches the one sketched on the pages of Julianna's journal—like a signature, almost, beginning with the day she wrote about seeing it on Orion's arm. The day that she said she knew something had changed in her.

"Did you paint it?" I ask him. It's an innocent enough question, but I watch closely for his reaction, because I think he's going to say no. Because I think I know who did.

"No," he says evenly. "My uncle brought it back for me from his last vacation."

He hasn't given me any reason to doubt his honesty. He told me the truth when I asked him about the sketch, but I don't believe him about this. That spiral in the corner has to be Julianna's. I search my memory for any mention she may have made of doing a painting for Orion. I don't recall anything, but that doesn't mean she didn't. Maybe that was what she meant when she said she tried to fix it. Maybe she went home and painted this, and wanted to give it to him. To see him again. Maybe she did, and that last entry wasn't the end of the story. And he's kept it all these years—his secret and hers.

"It's funny. I've never noticed it before," I say. "Is it new? Did he just give it to you?" Somewhere inside my head I realize I sound more like I'm interrogating than making polite conversation, but the questions come out before I can stop them.

"It's new to the wall," he says. "I just put it up a few days ago. But he brought it back from a trip last summer."

Now it feels like he's covering. "Trip to where?" I ask. "Where did he get it?"

He looks at me, mildly surprised, or maybe annoyed by my sudden interest. "Some little hippie town on the coast near Hearst Castle. I don't remember what it's called. He goes every year."

It's quiet as we both look at the painting again. And that's when I notice something else about it that cannot possibly be a coincidence. Or an accident.

"Anyway," he says, filling the silence, "I've got a lot to do before I close tonight."

He turns to go, and I know I should just leave it at that. Figure out exactly what I think is going on before I go any further or ask any more questions, but I can't stop myself. "Hey, Josh?" I say, though now it sounds wrong to me.

He pauses. Looks over his shoulder at me. "Yeah?"

"Did you ever notice the constellation in that painting?"

He glances at it, then back to me. Shakes his head. "No. You see one in it?"

I nod, making sure I look right at him. "I do. I see Orion."

## 16.

"A theory if you hold it hard enough
And long enough gets rated as a creed."
— "Etherealizing," 1947

By the time I burst through the double doors at school, sleep-deprived and wired on too much coffee, I've convinced myself that I'm either crazy or a genius because of where the words "what if" led me after I left Kismet yesterday. When I pointed out the constellation in the painting to Orion, he said nothing. He just dropped his eyes and ducked into the back room. I stayed then, leaving my chai untouched, listening to the rain pour down outside, and looking into the painting. The painting that had to have been done by her. All the while wondering—what if?

What if he wasn't hiding anything? What if he wasn't

lying about the painting? If his uncle really did bring it back from vacation? What would that mean?

And then—

What if there *is* more to the story? More than what I know, or what she wrote down. More—that happened after. What if I was the one who ended up with all the pieces to figure it out? Who was given the chance to see how they fit together? What if, after all these years, I found her journal for a reason. I know it's impossible to change the past, but what if I could uncover a version that's been hidden all this time. One that leads me to the most important question of all:

What if Julianna Farnetti is still alive?

I know it sounds insane. I'm still not sure how I'll be able to say this out loud, even to Kat. In the empty hallway, under the bad fluorescent lights, the question seems even more ludicrous in my mind. But then it doesn't. That "what if" kept me up all night, sent me to my computer to dredge up every article I could find on Shane and Julianna's wreck: the location of the Jeep in the icy river, the likelihood they'd been swept down it into the lake, where it was near impossible they'd ever be found. And then, the inarguable fact that they never were. That they disappeared into the swirling spring night, just like that. Case closed.

Or maybe not. Each time I tried to tell myself it wasn't possible, my mind went back to the painting hanging on the wall at Kismet. The palpable sadness in it, Orion visible in the sky, but mostly, the title. Frost's title. I'd remembered it being a sad poem, but when I got home, the first thing I did was open up my anthology to "Acquainted with the Night," and when I sat down to read his words, it was with a different set of eyes. As crazy as it sounds, I swear I could hear her voice in them.

> "I have been one acquainted with the night.
> I have walked out in the rain—and back in the rain.
> I have outwalked the furthest city light."

They're the words of someone who's been lost and lonely. Left something behind.

> "I have looked down the saddest city lane.
> I have passed by the watchman on his beat
> And dropped my eyes, unwilling to explain."

I see her in my mind, walking a lonely street, eyes downcast, hiding from her past someplace far from home. Maybe in that little artsy town where Josh's uncle found her painting, and where maybe . . . I can find her.

I can't let myself think that far ahead yet though. First I have to convince Kat to see what I see. I lean against her locker and wait, my mind buzzing and trying to fit something that I know will sound completely crazy into words that won't. But maybe it won't matter for her. Maybe she'll just go right along with it because it *is* so out there. She always goes more on possibility than logic. I'm usually the one bogged down in needing facts. And right now the fact that I see her coming down the hall with Trevor Collins, looking more than friendly, gives me pause.

They don't see me yet, but as I watch them walk they look . . . close. She leans into him and says something that looks like it surprises him before it sends a grin from one side of his face to the other, then tugs at my stomach. I'm surprised. I didn't think she . . . or he . . . I just didn't think they would ever—

I tell myself I don't have any right to be jealous. He's not mine, and I've passed up the opportunity more than once. And after the way I acted yesterday I wouldn't blame him if he stopped trying. But still. Why would *she* be so like that with him, when she knows I—I stop my tangent. Clearly I've had too much caffeine and too little sleep and am over-analyzing. Kat looks like she's flirting no matter what she does. Even when she says hi to me.

"Hey, you," she says with a smile.

I take a step forward to meet the two of them, loop my arm through Kat's, and words come out in one breathless rush. "Hey you guys, good morning, Kat can I talk to you alone?" I grab her arm.

They both look a little stunned.

"Morning to you too, Frost," Trevor says. He's still wearing a hint of the smile Kat put on his face with whatever she said. "Guess that's my cue to go." He gives Kat a look I can't read, winks at me, then turns and walks away from us without saying anything else.

"That was weird," I say.

She looks me over. "*You* were weird. What's going on? You look like crap."

I ignore the comment and pull her close so I can whisper. "I decided on my one thing."

"Huh?"

"My one *thing* I promised you I'd do." She's already looking at me like I've lost it and I haven't even told her what it is yet. "The unexpected *thing?*" Still nothing. I take a deep breath and try again. "You said I had to promise you I'd do one unexpected thing before graduation, and I have it."

Recognition slides over her face in a smile. "Oh yeeaah. What is it?"

"I can't tell you right now. It's a long story and I have to finish the last of the journals for Kinney. Come with me to the library."

She raises an eyebrow. "Look at you taking charge. It's too bad you didn't yesterday."

"What are you talking about?"

She ignores the question. "Never mind. Let's go. I haven't been to first period for the last four days. No need to break the streak now."

After a quick stop at Mr. Kinney's room to grab the box of journals, Kat and I find a seat at a table in the farthest corner of the library. She slaps another preprinted postage label on a manila envelope and tosses it in the box at our feet. "Okay. Let me repeat back to you what you just said so you can, you know, hear how insane you sound." I nod, pretty sure that this is part of the process of her agreeing to go with me.

"You, Parker Frost, stumbled across *and* stole Julianna Farnetti's journal from this stack here." She pats it and I nod. "Then you read it, found out she was in love with some other guy who wasn't Shane Cruz, but who you've decided is Josh from Kismet, and because of a tattoo and an anonymous painting in his café, you think Julianna Farnetti is still alive and it's your duty to reunite the two people who were actually meant to be together, by taking our unofficial senior trip to some art town instead of to San Francisco and the beach?" She stops to take a breath just in time for Ms. Moore to give her "the look," which Kat pointedly ignores. "It doesn't sound crazy at all, right?"

I don't answer right away. Instead I peel another postage label from the sheet to give Ms. Moore a chance to turn her attention back to her computer. Then I look at Kat. "Well, when you say it all dramatic like that . . ."

"You're insane." Kat peels and sticks another label. "And you've obviously read too much Nicholas Sparks."

"Ha. You have too. And you love this, I know it." She tries to hide a smile as she tosses another envelope into the box. "Kat, come on. It's exactly the type of thing you're always trying to get me to do."

"Go chasing after a dead girl? What about Shane? Where does he figure into this whole thing? Is he alive too?" She leans in close and lowers her voice to a sinister whisper. "Or did she kill him and run off?"

"*Kat*—" I stop. I haven't actually thought about where Shane fits into the puzzle. What the rest of his story is. "I don't know. But I'm taking this trip, and the only other person in the world I'd want to take it with is you. So you're coming. Right?" I try for the kind of confidence she usually throws at me, but it comes out as a question and a pathetic attempt at puppy dog eyes.

She rolls hers. "Of course I'll come, you dork. I just had to torture you a little. Make sure you're really committed to doing this thing."

"You *will*?" I jump out of my seat in a rush of relief and excitement and hope, and wrap my arms around Kat, not caring if Ms. Moore shoots another look our way.

"But you know you're gonna have to let me read the journal," she says. "Just in case you missed something important." She reaches around me for my backpack.

I grab it first. "Um . . . I—"

"Girls," Ms. Moore says with another pointed look, "I think it's time you get back to your classes. The period's almost finished, and it seems your work is too."

"Sorry," I say, slipping back into my normal, authority-fearing self. "You're right. We'll pack up right now." I lean across the table to gather up the various stacks of envelopes, and all in one motion Kat slides her hand into my open backpack, snatches out Julianna's journal, and slips it into her purse. I kick her under the table.

"Calm down," she smiles. "I'll give it back to you by the end of the day, and I won't show anyone. Promise."

Before I can answer her the bell rings and she spins on her heel and makes for the door, leaving me with the box to return to Mr. Kinney's and the hope beyond hope that she keeps her promise.

## 17.

"So all who hide too well away
Must speak and tell us where they are."
—"REVELATION," 1913

I'm waiting at Kat's locker after seventh period when I get her text: *Almost done w/journal. Holy. Shit. Meet me @ Kismet in an hour.*

This freaks me out for multiple reasons. First off, I know she's going to want to talk about it. At great length, and at a volume better suited for my house or hers than the place where the topic of conversation might actually be working. I'd trust her with my life, but I don't trust her not to interrogate Josh in a completely inappropriate manner.

I also know she won't change her mind or even answer if I text her back with a different place to meet. It's how she gets her way a lot of the time. By not giving people any other choice. The other thing that worries me when I walk outside is that her car is still in the parking lot.

I text her back: *Where are you??? Why an hour?*

I don't expect an answer, but I linger in front of the school just in case, watching the cars stream out of the parking lot and off into the warmth of the spring afternoon. Only when it's mostly emptied out do I really notice the other cars that are still there. With graduation only a few weeks away, most seniors are gone from campus after lunch, taking full advantage of their free period. Trevor always is. Not that I keep tabs on him, but I never see him at his locker after fifth period, so I'm pretty sure he leaves. Except he didn't today.

Today his Suburban is parked a few spaces away from Kat's truck, and he's nowhere to be seen either. Again that twinge of jealousy tugs at me, and I push away the foreign possibility that they could be together. I flash on how close they were in the hall this morning, what she said later about me not stepping up yesterday, and I check my phone again. No text.

I don't want to think about it. And I don't want to be mad at her when she shows up, because we have a lot of planning to do and only a few days to get it done. So instead of walking back in or texting her again, I get in my car and head over to Kismet, wondering if I really did miss my chance with Trevor, and hoping that she didn't decide to take it.

Josh is hanging a painting when I push through the door, and I very nearly turn around and walk right out.

"Be with you in just a sec," he says over his shoulder. He pushes up on his toes to get the frame in place high on the wall. Then he glances back at me. "Oh, hey. Come to order a chai you're not going to drink?"

"No." I force a laugh, but it comes out nervous. "I'm meeting my friend here for . . ." I stumble when he turns around and waits for me to finish. In the golden light of the afternoon I can see it again. That flash of him as Julianna saw him. "We're doing a project. Town history. Sort of."

"Exciting. Want something while you wait?" He smiles, and his eyes warm, and I can't help but imagine how they'd look if Julianna were the one who had walked through the door—if somehow I was right, and I could find her and tell her that he's been here all this time, and that I don't think he ever moved on. I'm getting ahead of myself, I know.

"Maybe just a water," I answer.

"Sure." He nods and walks back around the counter to grab me a bottle. I reach for my wallet, but he shakes his head. "Don't worry about it. You pretty much keep me in business these days."

"Thanks." I smile and take a nervous sip, awkward in the silence that follows.

"So what's your project about?" Josh asks. "The mine? History of the resort? What?"

I could lie and keep the conversation completely surface and safe, but he just gave me a wide open door for so much more than that. I decide to inch my toe over the threshold.

"No," I say carefully. "It's actually not for school. It's a lot more . . . important than that. I mean, it could be."

"Yeah?" He wipes down the spotless counter. I decide to go for it.

"You know that billboard at the edge of town? With the two kids who disappeared a long time ago?" He seems to tense, just slightly, but it passes quickly and I wonder if I imagined it.

"Sure," he answers. He ducks below the counter, comes back up with two packages of paper coffee cups even though the stacks already tower far above the register.

"Well, the girl—Julianna . . ." I pause and watch as he adds more cups to each stack without looking at me. "She left a journal." His hands stop moving, hover empty in the air between us. And now his jaw tightens and he avoids my eyes completely.

I take a step forward and lean across the counter so he has no choice but to look at me. "She wrote about a guy in it," I say, timidly at first. But then I get brave with what I know. "A guy that seems like he could've been you a long time ago. Except she called you Orion in her journal. She wrote about the first night you met, and how you made her feel like someone new, and how you swam in McCloud and sketched her on the beach, and kissed her under the stars—"

I stop, shocked at myself. Josh's face has gone white, and his eyes blink repeatedly in the silence that stretches dangerously tight between us.

The cups he's stacking topple. If they were glass, they'd

go crashing to the ground, shattering and sending shards flying in every direction, which is what it looks like has just happened inside of him.

"You loved her, didn't you?" My voice is barely above a whisper, and I have no idea where the nerve to say any of this is coming from, but it courses through me strong, like it's the truth, and as soon as I look at him I know it has to be.

Josh fixes his eyes somewhere beyond me, out the window and maybe all the way back to the past and to Julianna. I wait for him to answer. Bend to pick up the scattered paper cups. Hope that Kat doesn't walk in at that moment and give away the fact that I'm not the only one who knows. That I didn't keep their secret.

"She was . . ." Josh clears his throat. "She was one of those people that just kind of shine, you know? Everybody thought so." He smiles, but the edges of it are tinged with sadness. "She was just . . ." Finally, he looks at me. "Yeah, I loved her. Whatever that means when you're nineteen years old. From the second I met her I did, but—you already know she wasn't mine to love. And I don't think it was mutual."

The words *you're wrong* want so badly to burst out of my mouth, but I hold them back. He's leaned against the counter, arms crossed over his chest, and is now looking at me like he wants to keep talking. And I want to hear what he has to say.

"She told me that after a little while, and I was so messed up over it I just left town. I had to get out of here. I didn't tell her I was leaving or bother to say good-bye." He looks at the cups scattered over the floor. Chews his bottom lip for a moment. "But, um, I came back as soon as I heard. Drove all night long so I could help search and rescue, even though the last thing I wanted was to find her out in the snow or under the ice."

He pauses, and I can see he's gone back there in his mind. I picture him searching alongside everyone else, hoping for a miracle.

"I kept going out there for a long time after that, just looking for something. Even after they called off the search." He shakes his head and brings his eyes back to me, and now they're more contemplative than sad. "It was stupid, but I kept thinking that somehow she'd come back, because it didn't seem possible she was really gone."

He pauses and picks up a cup from the floor, turning it in his hands, and I want to tell him maybe he was right. I want to say what I've been thinking since yesterday. That even now, there could be a chance. A little thread drifting along out there in the ether, waiting to be connected to the story it belongs to.

He smiles tightly and sends the cup in his hands sailing into a nearby trash can. "Anyway."

I can tell by the shift in his tone he's about to end the conversation, but there's so much more I want to ask him. I want to know what made him tell me so much, why he didn't ask me more about the journal or how I got it, or what else I know. I want to ask him what he'd do differently if he could go back. And what he would do now if he could have another chance.

But the question that I say out loud is, "Why did you stay here? After."

He shrugs. "I probably should have left and moved on. Traveled, forgotten about it, let it go. But I kept staying and hoping, and eventually I opened this place and . . . that was it. Here I am." He spreads his hands out, then drops them to his sides like that's it. That's all there is to his story.

It's the saddest thing I've ever seen, and it's all I can do not to tell him everything I think right then and there, but fear holds me back. What if I'm wrong? What if I get his hopes up only to have them come crashing right back down?

The jingle of the bell above the door and Kat's voice keep me from having to decide.

"Parker! Good, you're here." She brushes past me, hardly registering Josh standing there. Her eyes search the walls. "Where's the painting? I need to see it."

"Kat—" I hope the tone I say it with is enough for her to understand that she needs to stop right now.

She does, and seems to suddenly notice that Josh is standing there looking from one of us to the other like he's waiting for an explanation of what the heck is going on. She looks him over carefully, her eyes wandering down the length of his arms. "Oh my God. Did she just tell you? Did she tell you what she thinks about the painting?"

"*Kat.*" This time I say it through gritted teeth, and since I know it's not enough, I grab her by the elbow and give her my best smile. "I need to talk to you. Outside. Now." I don't give her a chance to argue. Instead, I yank on her arm and usher us out the front door of the café, leaving an understandably confused-looking Josh inside.

"What are you *doing?*" I can barely contain my anger at her. "Why would you *say* that to him right now?"

"Why *wouldn't* I?" She shakes my hand off her arm. "Parker, I read the journal. She was totally in love with him, and he was with her, and they screwed it up. Don't you think he'd want to know if there's even the smallest chance that you're right?"

I glance inside, but Josh is nowhere to be seen. I don't blame him. "No," I say. "I don't think he'd believe me. As far as he's concerned, she's gone. It's a closed chapter of his life. I don't want to open it up with any false hope until I know for sure. I think he had enough of that the first time around."

"Are you *kidding* me? It's not a closed chapter of his life. He never got over her. That's why he is the way he is." Kat looks from me through the window of the café and back again. I don't say anything, and I don't move.

"Fine," she says finally. "But just so you know, you're ruining the picture I had in my mind of how this whole thing is going to go down."

"Really?" I laugh. "What did you have pictured?"

"Never mind. Can you follow me to my house? We have to figure out how we're gonna do this thing."

"Right. Let me just—" I stop short at what I see. "Is Trevor Collins sitting in your car?"

"Yeah." Kat dismisses the question with a wave of her hand. "Long story. I'll explain when we get there."

"Did you . . ." I don't want to finish the question.

"Yeah." She takes a step back. "I showed him the journal. He's coming with us. Meet me at my house, okay?"

She turns before I can argue, and when she gets in her car, Trevor Collins waves at me through the windshield. And now I know. I've lost my chance.

# 18.

"On Going Unnoticed"

—*1928*

I drive angry. When the light up ahead turns yellow, I hit the gas instead of slowing down, and by the time I fly through the intersection, it's definitely red. I don't care. I almost want to just keep going, right out of town. If it wasn't for the fact that Kat still has the journal, I might. Just go and take the trip by myself and forget about the fact that my best friend not only did the one thing I asked her not to by showing Trevor the journal, but she's also done a thing I didn't think I *needed* to ask her not to do. She had no right to show Trevor the journal. Or invite him on our trip. And now, all of a sudden, this . . . thing with him. I know I've said over and over I'm not interested, and I didn't think I was. Not really. But still.

I didn't expect her to make him her end-of-the-year fling. I thought she knew me better than that. Now I just feel like *I* should've known better.

I hit the gas again, hard. I don't know how I let this happen. How I let a real chance with him pass me right by. Especially now, with the end of school so close. I thought I liked the idea of possibility always floating there between us, but it's going to disappear soon, with graduation. I'll leave for school in the fall, and he'll head off to snowboard around the world, and the possibility that was there will dissolve into nothing without ever having a chance.

The next light is already red, and though I'm almost mad enough to sail right through the empty intersection, I slow down and come to a complete stop. And in that pause, when I finally take a breath, I know how I let this happen. I know exactly how. I did what I always do—deny and avoid and chicken out because I was scared of what might come next if I actually took a chance. A knot of regret tightens in my stomach, and frustration at myself and my continual inability to just *do* things. To just take risks or chances. Maybe if I had the words CARPE DIEM tattooed on my wrist I'd be different. Or WWKD—What Would Kat Do? That'd be a good one.

Ugh. It's too much to think about on top of the journal and Julianna, so I try not to. Instead, I turn the music up loud enough to drown everything out and drive the rest of the way to her house trying to sing along, even though I don't know the words to the song. By the time I pull into Kat's driveway, I've almost managed to focus all of my anger on the part about her showing him the journal and inviting him on our trip instead of on the other stuff that I don't want to think about right now, because being mad instead of hurt makes me feel a little stronger when I get out of the car.

Unfortunately, that strength lasts exactly the two seconds it takes for me to see Kat and Trevor in her living room window. They're sitting next to each other on the beige sofa. Close. She's smiling and talking away, and he's smiling too, eating up every second of it, I can tell. I know how her particular brand of charm works, and I'm sure he's just as helpless against it as every other male who comes into contact with her. I feel my jaw tighten, and have to fight the strong urge to just go home and leave them to their impulsive hook-up. But there's the journal I need to get back, at the very least.

It's this fact that forces my feet up the stairs of her front porch. I try to relax my face and concentrate on acting breezy and unaffected by Kat or Trevor or what might happen between the two of them. It'll be easy, I tell myself. I don't care anyway. He's a bad idea that I've said no to more than once. One who, if we actually went through with this trip, I'd be spending three days with, in a car, watching fall for my best friend.

My own tragic, unrequited love story.

I waver at the top stair. This plan gets worse every time I think about it, and with every second that passes, I'm more sure I can't go through with it. The conviction I felt after seeing the painting seems distant all of a sudden—like some dreamy, romantic notion that shouldn't have been more than a fleeting thought. Believing in anything more than that is likely a huge mistake—just like taking the journal and getting so caught up in it that I've ignored everything about my real life, including my speech.

The reality of it smacks me in the chest and spreads out heavy over my shoulders. The scholarship dinner, the night that could impact my whole future, is in four days, and I haven't written a single word of the speech that literally everything I've worked for depends on. I don't know what I was thinking. Taking a trip right now is not even a possibility for me, and that's what I need to tell Kat, as soon as I walk through the door.

"Hey," she chirps, when I open it. She jumps up from the couch in what seems like a suspiciously quick way to me, and I try to ignore all of the reasons my mind throws out as to why.

"Hey," I answer back. Grudgingly. I don't look at Trevor, not because I don't want to, but because now it feels like I can't without being completely transparent. I can feel disappointment etched onto my face.

I keep my eyes steady on Kat. "Listen. I was thinking on the way over here—this whole trip thing is a bad idea." I pause, and she gives Trevor a look. "It's stupid to think Julianna could still be alive somewhere. Or that she did that painting. Or that we could actually find her. I don't know what I was thinking. I got all excited reading her journal and—it was just . . . I *wasn't* thinking."

I pause again to give them a chance to agree, but they don't. I clear my throat. "And there's no way I could possibly go, anyway. I haven't even started my speech."

I can see Kat's trying to hide a smile, and the effort of it makes her look like she's about to burst. *"What?"* I ask, and it comes out sounding as frustrated as I feel.

"Really? You have to write your speech? Is that the best you can do? What you just said there?"

"I don't *need* to do any better than that," I snap. "It's important." Trevor shifts on the sofa and I soften my tone, not wanting to make him uncomfortable. "And I'd never get away with it anyway. It was a stupid idea. I'm embarrassed that I even came up with it in the first place." I glance in his direction, but keep my eyes on the floor, because that wasn't the only stupid idea I've had in the last few days.

Trevor nods slowly, taking a step toward me. "Hm. That's too bad, Frost. Because we found something in the art supply closet that might change your mind." This gets me. I look up at him. He smiles, and grabs something from behind the couch, stands up, and holds it behind his back. Then he moves in closer to me than he was before. "Something you might wanna see."

I step back, cheeks flaring up, but I don't look away from his blue eyes. There's something in them that really does make me want to see. "What are you talking about?" I ask. Curiosity has trumped my awkwardness. "What did you find?"

Kat doesn't wait for him to answer but jumps in, and her words tumble out in one ecstatic rush. "Okay. After I left the library I read the whole journal during second, and with all that stuff about art in there, it got me thinking that there might be something left of hers in the art supply closet because everyone knows Mr. Potter is a serious hoarder, so I asked Trevor for the keys and he wanted to know why, so I told him the whole thing and he offered to help. And then we found this."

Trevor pulls a canvas out from behind his back and puts it on display in his hands. "Voilà. A Julianna Farnetti original. Signed and dated. From before the crash."

I blink once, twice, three times. Then I let my eyes trail over the familiar lines of the Minarets and the sky behind them. It's almost the same painting as in the cafe, but less complex, without the sharp emotion or sophistication of the other one. Like an earlier draft. I stare at the blank space in the sky where the stars outline the constellation Orion in the painting in Kismet. This was before everything. Before she met him. Before she had to make a choice that didn't feel right and lied to do what she thought was. Before the sadness of *Acquainted with the Night*. I swallow hard and bring my eyes down to the bottom corner. Her signature is there in this one, scrawled out in the same swirly, hopeful hand as it is on the front of her journal, which Kat is now holding up next to it.

"Can you *believe* it?" Kat can barely contain herself. "What are the *chances*? That's why I wanted to see the painting so bad when I got there today—to compare them—but you yanked me out of there like a crazy person."

"I'm sorry," I whisper. "I didn't want you to say anything to Josh yet." I can't take my eyes off the painting. "This is amazing, I—" I simultaneously forgive her and feel like the world's worst friend for jumping to the worst possible conclusion about her and Trevor and what they were doing together. "I am an idiot."

"Actually," Trevor says, handing it to me, "I think you might be kind of a genius for putting it all together." He smiles when he says it, and I melt a little inside.

Kat jumps in front of him again. "So like I was saying. It's her. It has to be her. It's fate, and they're supposed to be together, like you said. Like in all your sappy-ass movies."

The doubt and worry from a few moments ago try to hold on, but everything in me wants to agree and run with this idea. I look down at the painting in my hands. "I don't know . . ."

I look at her name in the corner of the canvas, and in that moment I'm sure. For some reason this is the one unexpected, important thing I'm supposed to do.

"Come on," Kat says. "We're doing this. We're going to find Julianna Farnetti and reunite her with her one true love, and it will be brilliant and beautiful and the best thing you've ever done. I've got it all planned out. There aren't very many little art towns around Hearst Castle, and I found one that seems promising. It's called Harmony." She gives a nod of finality and skips the part where either one of us get to respond, then continues, all business.

"So I think we should go with my original, brilliant plan to use Senior Ditch Day. It's the perfect cover. You'll get up and act like everything's normal. Pack your stuff in your backpack, park your car at school, then walk to the Carl's Jr. parking lot."

"Of course." I have to laugh at this, because in our little town, Carl's Jr. was somehow established as the official meeting place for anything. My theory is that it was before cell phones, when everyone had to actually meet up somewhere to find out what was going on and where the parties were. Now it's like a Summit Lakes teenager tradition. Meet at Carl's Jr.

"We'll all meet there," Kat says. Then she nudges Trevor. "Right?"

"Yep," he nods. "Bright and early."

"He's driving," Kat says. "Your car needs to stay at school, mine would never make the trip, and it's never bad to have a guy along for this type of thing, anyway."

Trevor smiles. "And I thought you were only using me for my car. Happy to know it's me you might actually need." Kat ignores him, and though I'm still unclear on exactly why he's coming along, I attempt to do the same, which doesn't really work. That smile, and those eyes—

"Parker—you listening?"

I nod and make a conscious effort to look only at Kat.

"Okay. So we'll pick you up and get on the road, and we'll have a head start since the entire senior class will be gone. I don't think they even bother calling parents that day. Then, 'after school,' you just call your mom and tell her you'll be at my house for the night. My mom's working a double so she won't be home to answer, and we'll be back by Tuesday afternoon before your mom has a clue you were ever gone, and in time for your dinner thing the next day."

"But what about—"

"Your speech? Easy. Write it this weekend, and you can practice it in the car, all the way there and back."

"But my mom—she's never gonna say yes to me staying at your house that night."

Kat sighs, then steps in front of me and puts her hands firmly on both my shoulders. "Then make something up. Or just do it anyway. At some point, you're gonna have to stand up to her and just do what you want. I can't think of a better reason to than this."

I take a deep breath, then let it out slow. She's right. And in theory this should all work, but I know my mom well enough to guess that it probably won't. Not only is my mom aware of where I am at all times, she also seems to possess the ability to predict when I'm even *thinking* of doing something I shouldn't. On the other hand, she *has* been even more wrapped up in work than normal over the last few weeks, so maybe her guard is down. Or she's distracted enough, at least. It's only one night.

"Okay," I say. And it makes me panic a little inside, so I take another deep breath. "Let's do it."

"Really? Goddamn, I'm proud of you, P!" Kat smacks me on the butt. "Now go home and act normal and write your speech."

"Okay," I say again, not only because she dove whole-heartedly into this idea with me, but she's figured out a way to actually do it. To make something happen. And I'm grateful to her for that. Almost grateful enough to quelch the tiny, questioning voice in the back of my mind that keeps trying to figure out how Trevor fits into all of this. Or maybe where I fit in with him. Either way, sharing the small space of his car for a little while *might* not be the worst thing ever.

Kat hands me Julianna's journal. "Here, I almost forgot. Since you're the one who figured this out, you're going to be the one to give it back when we find her. Keep it safe until then. Now go. Be all studious and obedient this weekend so your mom doesn't suspect anything." She steps past me, opening the door wide for me to go. And then she glances from me to Trevor and back. "And give this guy a ride home while you're at it."

## 19

"Into My Own"

—*1915*

"So . . . which way are we going?" I say over my shoulder as I back out of Kat's driveway. Despite all my Facebook research, I don't actually know where Trevor lives.

His eyes catch mine when I turn back to the steering wheel. "I don't know," he says with a smile. "Which way *are* we going, Frost?"

His tone and the question send a shot of nervousness straight to my stomach, but with everything that just happened, I'm feeling bold. I put the car in park, turn to face him, and shrug, trying to keep from smiling back. "That really depends on where you *want* to go, Trevor Collins."

His smile broadens at this, and he unbuckles his seat belt

and turns so he's facing me. And we sit, with my car idling, and the music playing, just looking at each other, and there's so much there, wanting to be said. And done. All I would have to do at this moment is lean across the electric space between us, and—

And in one smooth motion, Trevor does. I freeze, and then I'm leaning too, eyes closing, to meet him halfway for this thing we've been dancing around forever. But I don't feel his lips on mine. Instead, I feel his mouth next to my ear, and his breath warm on my neck, not one part of us actually touching. "You're the one driving," he says, "so really it's up to you."

Wounded pride burns in my cheeks. I don't want it to be all up to me. Why does it have to be? I don't move, and neither does he, at first. Fine. I can play this game too.

"In that case, " I say, and I shock myself by letting my lips brush his neck when I do, "then I guess I should take you home, since you don't seem to have anywhere else to go."

I don't know who's more surprised at this, me or him. But when he leans back shaking his head, confident smile in place, and I see the flush in his cheeks too, it makes me feel better. I put the car back in drive and grab the wheel with both hands so he won't see that they're still shaky. And then I'm the one who smiles. "So why don't you tell me how to get there."

I take the long, long way home after I drop him off, partly because I want to hold on to the nervous, exhilarated feeling that's still there, and partly because I need to focus on our plan, which hinges on me writing my speech over the weekend, and somehow finding the guts to completely disobey my mom if I need to. That's the part that makes me the most nervous.

By the time I walk through the front door, I've almost got myself convinced that if I find Julianna, it'll all be worth it. And then I hear it in her voice.

"Parker? I need to talk to you."

It's that tone I hate. The one that's stern and trying to remain calm but is clearly having trouble doing it because she's pissed about something. I run through the possibilities of what it could be. I haven't done anything. Yet. I slide my bag off my shoulder and walk over to her as casually as I can.

She's sitting at the dining room table, fingers clacking away on her laptop.

"What's up?" I ask, a touch too high-pitched. "How's the shop going? That order come in on time? I can help process it next week if you want." Maybe if I just keep talking I can get her off topic and off my back about whatever it is.

"Did you run a red light today?" she asks without looking up.

*Would you be asking me if I didn't?* God, I can't do anything in this town without someone telling on me to her. "Yes," I admit, because it's no use lying. I'm probably on camera. Or she has multiple witnesses. "I'm sorry. I wasn't paying attention and—"

"That's what I wanted to talk to you about." She closes her computer with a neat snap and looks at me very carefully, eyes intent on something. "Is everything all right with you,

Parker? You've seemed very distracted lately, like you're all of a sudden losing focus." She pauses. "Now is *not* the time to lose focus." She's quiet again, and I know she's winding up to ask the big question I don't want to have to answer. I try desperately to think of a way to change the subject before she can do it, but I'm not quick enough.

"I'd like to see your speech. Is it finished?"

"It's—almost. But I'm not ready for you to look at it yet. I need the weekend to go over it."

She eyes me, weighing my words. I've never given her any reason not to trust me, but I can see she's not convinced, and I realize why. I probably sound like my dad to her right now.

"I just want to fix a few things before I show you," I say. "I'm going to work on it all weekend, and I promise you can see it when I'm done."

A few seconds that feel like an eternity pass before she answers. "Okay. But you're not going anywhere until I have your speech. Finished. Got it?" Her eyes go big while she waits for an answer.

"Got it," I say, because that's what she expects me to do. I swallow hard. Nervousness at what I have planned flutters in my stomach, but today something is different. Today I have a reason that's worth enough to step out from under her thumb and take a chance. I just need to write that speech.

I wait a moment to see if there's anything else, but she seems satisfied. I take a step back. "Okay, then. I'm gonna head up and get to work."

"Good," she says. "Good girl." And then she opens up her laptop again as if it's all settled, and I'm glad, because I'm sure that if she actually looked at my face she'd see everything I am about to do.

I don't actually breathe again until I'm up in my room with my door closed. It's a funny thing, my almost morbid fear of my mom. She's never intentionally mean, and she doesn't yell. And she's always been supportive of whatever I've done. But I've always done what she wanted. I haven't ever disappointed her. That's what it is. That's what I'm afraid of doing. Because that's what my dad did over and over, and I saw what happened then.

When he tried and failed, again and again, to write his second book, she saw things in black and white—he needed to suck it up and move on. Support his family. Be a grown-up. Stop chasing something that eluded him, no matter how much it meant. She wanted a life of stability and practicality, one she could depend on. He wanted a life of creativity and inspiration, one he could find his voice in. And neither one could understand how what they wanted wasn't enough for the other.

So he left, and I became careful about what I said I wanted. Grades and awards and teacher recommendations became my way to ensure my mom's approval. AP classes, extra credit, and concrete accomplishments. They're the things she values, as opposed to the things she associates with my dreamer of a father. I've worked at it and worked at it, and now I'm at the end of high school and I have all of those things, including her approval. But right now, what

I really want is something that means something to *me*. Something that I believe in, and that I do because I want to, not because I think it'll prove something to my mom.

I don't know how to begin to write my speech, or if I even want to if it's just another attempt to prove myself to her. But I do know that, come Monday, I'll be on the road, somewhere between who I've always been and who I want to be.

## 20.

### "The Courage to Be New"
#### —1947

The girl I want to be tries to look casual standing in front
of Carl's Jr. at six a.m., wearing a huge backpack and irratio-
nally scanning the parking lot for any sign of my mom bran-
dishing the speech I'd pieced together from a Google search
of "inspirational speeches" and left on the kitchen table for
her approval. It was a Hail Mary. I'd spent the entire weekend shut away in my room, trying to come up with words
I believe in, that the scholarship committee would believe
in too, but I kept coming up blank. Instead of writing my
speech, I went back to other words—Julianna's, and Robert
Frost's, and even my dad's. So when Sunday evening rolled
around, I did what I had to do in the hopes that somewhere

on the road ahead of me, I'd find what I really wanted to say.

I check my phone again, hoping for a *We're on our way* text from Kat, but no such luck.

The girl I actually am is a nervous wreck who is totally unsure about the trip, hesitant to really hope we'll find Julianna, all mixed up about what may or may not be going on with Trevor, and petrified of how much trouble I'm guaranteed to be in when I get home. I try not to think about all that, though. I lean my back against the building and look out over the ring of mountains that surrounds our little town, hoping to channel some of the calm of the morning. The air is a touch cooler than is comfortable in the cutoffs and tank top I threw on in a hurry, so I pull a sweatshirt out of my bag and slip it over my head.

Though it's still shadowed where I'm standing, the peaks of the mountains are washed golden by the rising sun, and cloudless blue sky stretches out in every direction. Spring is undeniably here, and with it that feeling of newness and possibility and freedom. A fresh start, which is exactly what I want. I want this day to be my fresh start. I want this to be the day I step out of my comfort zone and go somewhere new. I've got the small amount of cash I've saved up, my MapQuest printouts, the journal, and my dad's signed copy of Robert Frost's collected poems tucked into my bag. Somehow the combination of those things feels right. I have no idea what I will do or even say if we actually find Julianna, but I'm ready. Ready for whatever happens.

As if cued by my last thought, Trevor's Suburban turns into the parking lot and crosses the empty spots to where I'm standing. Kat waves excitedly from the front seat, and Trevor gives a nod and a half smile before he puts the car in park. For a second it crosses my mind that it's strange they showed up together, but that thought is overshadowed by a second one: *Holy crap, we're really doing this.*

They both get out, and Kat crashes into me in a sort of tackle hug. "Holy shit, Parker, we're really doing this! God, I'm so frickin' proud of you! You have the journal? And the map, and everything?" I nod as best I can, my answer muffled by her cleavage and enthusiasm. She releases me. "Good. I'm gonna go grab us some food. I'm starving. You want coffee?"

"Um, sure. You want me to come with you?"

"No. You stay. I'll be right back," she says with a wink and a glance at the Suburban. She pushes through the red double doors, releasing a waft of grease and coffee from inside, and then she's gone. When I turn back to the car, Trevor gets out casually, his hair still morning messy, which is adorable, and his eyes as blue and bright as ever.

"Morning, Frost," he says with a grin that seems either a little shy or a little tired, I can't tell which. He holds an arm out. "Let me get that bag for you."

I slide it off my shoulders and hand it to him. "Thanks."

"Wow," he says, hefting it up and down a couple of times. "Kat didn't tell me we were running away forever. You bring all your earthly possessions along?"

That familiar warmth creeps up my neck and threatens to spread out over my cheeks. "No. I just . . . I didn't know what I would need, so I brought it all. You never know what the weather will be like on the coast. Sometimes—" *Oh my God,*

*just be quiet now. Stop being lame. Be someone new today. Brave. Bold.*
"Yeah, I guess I probably brought too much."

"That's okay." Trevor hefts my bag into the back of his Suburban. "Just giving you a hard time."

He shuts the trunk and we both slide our hands into our pockets at the same time. He takes his out. I laugh. What happened to who we both were yesterday, in my car?

"So," Trevor says, after an awkward moment. "Is she always this . . . peppy in the morning?" We both look through the window to where Kat is inside gesturing wildy and the guy behind the counter is laughing.

I turn back to him. "Not usually. I think it's because she's finally getting me to do something crazy, that she would do. That *I* normally wouldn't."

"Ah," he nods. "Corrupting the indomitable Parker Frost. It *is* an accomplishment, actually."

"Indomitable? That's a big word for you, Trevor Collins." He laughs, and it's enough to encourage me. "It might be an accomplishment," I say. "But she's been failing at that for years. There's a chance I'm just a lost cause."

Trevor raises an eyebrow. "I don't know about that, Frost. Maybe you just haven't been tempted with the right transgression yet."

*Brave. Bold. WWKD.*

"Or maybe I have," I say with a smile I'm pretty sure looks like one Kat would give. "Maybe I just haven't made up my mind whether to risk it."

He smiles slow and leans in close. Close enough to touch. "That's too bad. Because all the fun is in the risking."

"Then maybe you should try it some time," I answer back.

Kat comes out then, loaded up with more grease-dotted bags than it would take to feed all of us three times. She sees me looking. "*What?* Road trip food doesn't count."

"True," Trevor says. "Let's get on the road. So we can eat some of that food that doesn't count."

With that we pile into Trevor's car—which he informs us is actually called the Silver Bullet. Kat hops in the back, and I, by Kat's design, I think, sit shotgun. Seat belts click, the familiar chorus of "Should I Stay or Should I Go" rushes out of the speakers, and greasy fast food breakfast is distributed all around.

Kat raises her Diet Coke in between me and Trevor. "To fate, friendship, and adventure. Here we go!" We tap our drinks together. Trevor puts his arm on the back of my seat to twist himself around when he backs up, and when he does, our eyes catch.

"Wait," I say.

"No backing out now," he says. "You're committed."

"No, it's not that. I'm not backing out. There's just one place we have to stop before we really get on our way."

"Let me guess," Kat says. "Summit Lake?"

I turn around. "How did you know?"

"You might be the one with the scholarship to Stanford," she says through a mouthful of breakfast burrito, "but I'm always one step ahead of you."

## 21.

> "But if I had to perish twice,
> I think I know enough of hate
> To say that for destruction ice
> Is also great
> And would suffice."
> —*"FIRE AND ICE," 1920*

The road to Summit Lake is off the main highway, fifteen minutes or so out of town, and is definitely out of our way, but there's no other place this trip should begin. If we're searching for a different ending to Julianna's story, we need to start where the original version ended. When Trevor makes the turn off the highway, the road narrows as if that's the only way it can manage to hug the side of the mountain it puts us on. We all kind of go quiet when we round the first turn and the view unfolds in front of us, grand and dramatic, and in my mind, a bit sinister, too.

The edge of the road may as well be the edge of the earth, the drop is so sheer. When I was little, I'd cower in the back with my hands over my eyes on roads like this, scared that the slightest shift of the steering wheel would send us right off the edge. Today I look out my window, first across to the other side of the gorge, which is thick with the green of aspen trees, and then down, down, down to the bottom, where icy snowmelt flows, fast and unforgiving. The sight of it makes me doubt everything I've come up with about the possibility of Julianna still being alive. It would take more than a miracle to survive the plunge from the road to the bottom of the gorge.

"I wonder what the hell they were doing out here," Kat says from the back seat. "You know? This road is scary enough in broad daylight, with no snow on it."

"Maybe it was an accident they ended up here," Trevor says. "Everyone's always said he was drunk when they left. Maybe they were trying to go out to the Grove or something and got confused. Who knows?" He shrugs, but keeps both hands firm on the steering wheel, his eyes never leaving the road as we wind around another curve. There could be a million different reasons, but there's no one to ask.

We pass a yellow sign that says SCENIC OVERLOOK, with a picture of a camera on it, and then the dirt turnout it refers to. "Maybe they were looking for a place to talk . . . or park," I say. "Like one of these spots." It's not an uncommon thing for kids in our town to go driving out into the boonies to "talk." There are plenty of awe-inspiring spots with views that people go out to under the pretense of looking at them.

Kat leans forward on my seat. "I bet she told him about Orion that night—at the party, and that's why they left. And then maybe they got in a fight, and he drove out here. That could happen if you were drunk and pissed off. "

"Yeah." I nod. "It probably could." I shiver a little at the thought of Julianna telling Shane on this road. In a snowstorm, when he'd been drinking. Finding out something like that might make it easy, in a moment of hurt or anger, to turn the steering wheel just enough to do something you could never take back.

We round another curve and pass another SCENIC OVERLOOK sign, and the view from this one really is worthy of the title. From this vantage point you can see where the icy water of the river tumbles into the lake and then disperses into the stillness of it almost immediately, like it's been swallowed by the depth and the cold. Summit Lake is one of the deepest in the country, breathtakingly beautiful, and the quintessential summer image of our town. Every Summit Lakes postcard or calendar has a shot of this lake, a blue-green gem nestled at the base of glacier-carved granite mountains. It's dramatic, and striking, but to me it's always been a distant, cold, kind of beautiful. It's a place with a history of tragedy. Shane and Julianna are just one chapter.

The road begins its descent as it wraps around to the south shore of the lake. We pull into the empty parking lot, and Trevor parks facing the water, then cuts the engine and is quiet a moment. Kat is too for once, and I think it's because we're all sitting here looking at the water, half in the shadow, half in the sun, thinking about Julianna Farnetti. I am. I'm wondering whether she's beneath its surface, deep in the blue water so dark it looks black, together forever with Shane Cruz, like she was supposed to be according to everyone else; or whether she somehow escaped that fate, slipped out of the lake, and found her way to a new life, far away from here and from who she was before.

"Shall we?" Trevor asks.

I nod.

We all open our doors to get out, and when we shut them, the sound echoes off the sharp, sheer ridges of granite, like three muted shots. Then silence. Kat hugs her arms to her chest. "God, this place gives me the creeps."

"Can't imagine why," Trevor says. "Between those kids that fell through the ice and the guys who tried to save them, and Shane and Julianna, it's got its fair share of ghosts floating around." He grins. "No pun intended."

He's right. It's one of those places steeped in stories that go back even past our childhoods. There was a girl, probably around Julianna's age, whose dad drowned in this lake, along with a school bus driver, when they both tried to save four boys who had walked out onto the ice and fallen through. Before that there was a bloody shoot-out between a group of escaped convicts and the sheriffs who'd chased them there—one that ended with the sheriffs being dumped in the lake and supposedly haunting its shores for years after. And long before that there was the legend of a Paiute boy who disrespected the lake's power and was swallowed by the water, never to be seen again.

"Ha. Ha." Kat rolls her eyes, then runs them over the surface of the water. "Funny, except nobody floats here. They all sink to the bottom, then slip down the center of the hourglass." She shivers. "Ugh. You couldn't pay me all the money in the world to go swimming in this lake. For exactly that reason."

"Oh, come on," Trevor says. "The bottom is so far down there, I'm sure they're all long gone now."

"Okay, that's enough." Kat turns to me. "Why did we need to come here again?"

"I just wanted to see if . . . if there's anything else here to find out. Or . . . I don't know." I look across the glass surface of the water, blue-green around the edges and in the places the sunlight has reached. The rest of the water is a nameless color so dark it gives nothing away. It just reflects all my questions back, sharp and impassive, like a mirror. The stillness of it is unnerving. Like it's holding its breath, waiting for us to do something.

"Come on," I say. "Let's walk. I think there's a memorial near those trees." I point to a cluster of aspens at the lake's edge and we cross the parking lot.

There's a narrow trail that follows the wavy edge of the lake, dotted with forest service signs detailing the history and geology of it. They're the types of signs only tourists and old people usually stop to read, but while Kat and Trevor walk on, I linger at the first one. It's a series of pictures showing how the surrounding mountains burst out of the ground as a result of fiery volcanoes, and then the canyons and gorges between them were carved out and scoured over thousands of years by slow-moving glaciers. Its title is "Fire and Ice." Like the Frost poem, and a line from Julianna's journal about the night she and Orion went to the hot springs and kissed under a blanket of stars. I make a mental note to look the actual poem up when we get back to the car. It seems fitting that there's a reference here. Her world, the one that she knew, with Shane as her constant, ended with fire—the desire for Orion. And then it ended again, here, in the ice of the river and lake. Or maybe it didn't.

I jog a few steps to catch up to where Kat and Trevor have stopped. I was right about the memorial. Raised up from the ground on a cement platform is one of those oversize, bronze plaques. It has a permanent vase at the top, filled with snowy white flowers, which I'm sure are kept up by the Cruz family, who probably also installed the memorial. The inscription below the vase reads:

> In loving memory of
> Shane Cruz
> and
> Julianna Farnetti,
> Two stars
> Whose light was gone too soon.

I read it over two more times, focusing on the words and wondering if Josh has ever come out here and what he must've thought when he looked at those words. I can't imagine what it must've been like for him in the beginning, not to be able to show the depth of his grief for her or what it meant. Not to be acknowledged as someone who lost her. If I were him, I don't think I would've ever come out here. I would've stayed away, and then, if I wanted to go somewhere to feel near to her, I'd go to McCloud, which even I thought of now as their special, secret place.

"So what do you think, Frost?" Trevor says. "Is she here? Or are we going to find her?"

"We're gonna find her," Kat says. "I know we are."

I glance down at the plaque, then out over the lake, trying to feel what I really believe. "I don't know," I say softly. And it's the truth. I really can't say.

"Well then," Trevor replies, "let's get on the road and go find out."

Kat squeezes her arms tighter to her chest and nods. "Yeah. Let's get going. This is pretty and meaningful and all that crap, but I've had enough of this place."

"You guys go ahead. I'll be there in a minute," I say.

"You all right?" Kat asks.

"Yeah, yeah, I just want to stay another minute. I'll meet you at the car."

"Whatever you say."

She and Trevor turn and head back down the trail in the direction we came from. I watch for a moment, half-curious if I'll see a glance pass between them or her hand on his arm—something that might explain why she invited him to come along, but there's nothing. I look back over the still surface of the lake like maybe I'll hear something if I listen close enough. But the only sound comes from the other side where the river meets it in a constant hush. An indistinguishable whisper.

*Don't be here, under the water,* I say to her in my mind. *Don't be a lost love for Orion. Be a miracle. Be alive, and living a beautiful life somewhere new, however impossible it seems. Let me find you because I'm supposed to, and because you're supposed to be with him. Not just a distant memory. Let me find you so that this means something.*

Kat's voice echoes off the granite mountains, interrupting my prayer/plea. "Parker! Come on! We're losing road time!"

"Coming!" I shout back.

I take one last look at the lake and decide that we'll find her. That it's meant to be. And then I turn and run for Trevor's car where he, Kat, and fate are waiting for me.

## 22.

"Peril of Hope"
—*1961*

Three hours down the empty two-lane highway, I'm happy that it's leading us to the coast at least, because after passing through the familiar string of one-blink towns named after various types of pine trees, we are traveling down a stretch of road so barren and plain it's hard to feel like we're making any progress at all.

"We should've brought snacks," Kat says from the back. "It's ridiculous to be on a road trip without snacks. I could use some candy right now. And a Diet Coke. And maybe some chips. Those spicy red ones that make your face sweat." She leans forward, resting her elbows on mine and Trevor's seats. "When's the next place to stop?"

Trevor points at a sign as we pass. "Casa Junction, in another sixty-two miles."

"Well, could you give it a little gas, then? I'm starving."

I turn around. "How can you be hungry? You ate two breakfasts."

Trevor glances down at the speedometer. "I'm already doing eighty."

"I have a fast metabolism," Kat says. "Apparently faster than Trevor Collins here is willing to drive."

He laughs at this and I feel the car accelerate.

"Eighty's fast enough," I say. "The last thing we need is a ticket."

"Fine." Kat sits back in her seat, all huffy. I rummage through my purse for something to give her, because I know all too well what happens when she goes too long without eating. "Here," I tell her. "Here's a piece of gum. Will that last you sixty-two miles?"

"Maybe," she says, taking it. "But you've been warned. I'm bitchy when I'm hungry."

"As opposed to other times?" Trevor asks, with a side glance and a quick smile at me.

Kat kicks the back of his seat and laughs. "Shut up. The only reason I'm nice to you is because of my friend up there in the front seat."

My cheeks flare up and I turn to look far away, out the window. I'm ridiculously relieved by Kat's comment, and once again feel like a bad friend for being so paranoid about her and Trevor.

"What's that supposed to mean?" he asks.

"Nothing," I say quickly. I reach for the volume knob and turn up the radio, which is tuned to some XM station I've never heard of, and none of us say anything for a long moment. Then Trevor speaks up.

"So. Parker. You thought about how you're gonna approach this? Like, if we walk into an art gallery, and Julianna Farnetti is standing there in all her perfect, golden glory, do you know what you're gonna say to her? Because it's probably safe to assume that if she's stayed hidden this long, she's not gonna be happy about being found, you know?"

Kat sits up all of a sudden. "Or—oh my God, what if Shane's there too? What if they staged the whole thing and ran off together and have been living a secret life ever since?"

"Why would they have done that?" I ask. "That doesn't make any sense."

"And your theory about just Julianna surviving does?"

"More than both of them still being alive," Trevor says. "He didn't have any reason to run away. She kind of did." He's right. If she did, and has stayed away all these years, why on earth would she ever want to be found?

Panic zips through me. I hadn't thought of that at all. Actually, I haven't thought about anything past the idea of finding her, which, as much as I hope to, still seems unlikely. But if I really do, and I tell her about Orion, who's to say she'd actually come back? And if she did, who's to say he'd want her to? Who's to say they'd actually end up together? Or that they should? What if, by doing this, I'm disrupting the way things were *actually* meant to be, as sad as they are?

It's hard to make the distinction between believing I'll find her and using the search for her as an excuse to finally set out and do something different. The prospect of having to actually say something to her, and where to begin coming up with the right thing to say, is almost enough to make me want to turn around and go home. Sit in my room and obediently write my speech, and go on with my uneventful and safe, predictable, planned-out life. I shake my head. "I have no idea what I'll do or say if we find her. None."

"Hm." Trevor nods, but doesn't add anything.

Silence settles over the three of us, filled in only by the background music and the barren desert scenery zipping by outside the window. I try to picture actually walking into the gallery and finding Julianna there. I see her standing to the side of a painting, maybe talking to a potential buyer who has fallen in love with one of her pieces. She doesn't notice me at first, which gives me a chance to watch and observe just how much she's changed, and how much is still the same. I don't remember ever hearing her voice, but I haven't ever forgotten her face—the high, delicate cheekbones, the olive skin and green eyes, the cascade of wavy golden hair. I picture it all still the same, only more beautiful in real life than it is in the photographs and on the billboard. And that's as far as I get. What comes next? How do you approach someone who's pretended to be dead for ten years? What do you open with?

"Okay," Kat says, interrupting the thought. "I think if we find her, you just walk in and hand her the journal," Kat says, as if she can read my mind. "That way she can't pretend not to be who she is. The shock alone would give her away."

"And then what?" I turn to Kat.

"And then . . . let her do the talking. See what she says. That's all you *can* do because you can't guess how she's gonna react to being found."

Kat's probably right, but I don't do wait-and-see very well. I like to have a plan to follow. "Okay, so what if she gets mad and tells me to leave?"

"Don't."

"What if she pretends she has no idea what it is?"

"Then bring up Orion. Tell her that he went back to town and has been there, pining for her ever since. Read to her from the journal. Anything. You're only gonna get one chance with this, so you better make it count."

"What if she's not there at all?" I ask. "What if I'm wrong, and she really is in Summit Lake, down in the bottom of the hourglass?"

"Then you took a chance on something for once. You did something you wouldn't normally do, and that's what matters. Right, Collins?"

Trevor's been quiet this whole time, maybe thinking of different scenarios on his own, but now he nods. "It's true." He glances at me again. "Taking a chance can be worth a lot more than you know." He puts his eyes back on the road— the one in front of us that's unknown and wide open. The road less traveled. And somehow I think he's not just talking about this trip. There's something in his voice that goes straight to my stomach and sends a warm tingly feeling right through the rest of me.

"I hope so," I answer. And now I'm not just talking about the trip either. There are a few other things I've decided to take a chance on in these two days of my one wild and precious life.

## 23.

"Accidentally on Purpose"
—1960

Fifty-seven minutes later we pull into Casa Junction, a rest stop complete with gas, an extensive food mart, and a sprawling grassy area where people can let their kids run around and their dogs do their business. Kat leaps from the car and makes for the mini-mart and the bathroom, Trevor gets out, pops the gas cap, and takes the nozzle from the pump. I climb from my seat and stretch in the sun. It's not even noon yet, and we've hit the halfway mark. The air here is already warmer than it will be at home today, and this little thing feels like a gift. I pull my sweatshirt up over my head, and when I lean over to put it in the car, I catch Trevor watching me. He smiles, slow, and like he wants to say something.

"What?" I ask, instantly self-conscious. This morning, in the dim light of my bedroom, I was feeling confident and optimistic and daring. Daring enough to throw on one of Kat's little tank tops and a pair of cutoffs I'd ordinarily never wear out of the house because they're so short. Now I feel like I'm dressed up as someone else. Someone far more sure of herself than I feel at the moment.

"Nothing," Trevor answers with that same smile. He turns and watches the numbers roll over on the gas pump, and I fidget with my shorts and sneak a downward glance to make sure my bra's not showing or anything.

"Um . . . I'm gonna go get something to drink inside. You want anything?" I try to sound casual and confident instead of like I wish I was wearing something else.

"Sure." He looks at me again—really looks at me—and I fight the urge to throw my sweatshirt back on. "I'll take a Coke and a pack of Starburst, since you're offering." I nod and start to back away, but he stops me. "Hey, Frost."

"Yeah?"

"You look good today."

Normally, with him, I would toss back a little sarcasm and brush off the comment as disingenuous. Especially after our little moment in my car. But after he says it he clears his throat, looks down, and kicks something on the ground. Almost like *he's* all of a sudden self-conscious.

"Thanks," I say simply. I can't hide the smile it puts on my face, so I turn and head for the store without saying anything else, and I hope he's watching me as I walk away, because after that, I'm sure there's just a little strut in my step.

Inside the empty store it's not hard to find Kat. She's in the candy aisle, plucking a rainbow of packages from the racks like she's picking berries or something.

"So," she asks as she examines the remaining candy on the shelves. "Did you guys have a moment out there?"

I laugh. "What are you talking about? No." She just looks at me, and I look over my shoulder and through the window to where I can see Trevor now washing the windshield with a squeegee. "Maybe. Sort of. Were you watching?"

She breaks into a wide smile, unwraps a red Tootsie Pop, and pops it in her mouth. "Maybe. Nice outfit, by the way. Glad to see you finally owning your hotness, even if it is a little late." She beams like a proud mother. "He watched you walk all the way over here, and I watched you look all giddy and nervous about it."

"I looked nervous?"

"Only from the front. I'm sure you looked just fine from behind," she says with a wink. "Good. My genius plan is working."

"What genius plan?"

"I love you, P, but for a smart person you can be awfully dense sometimes."

"*What?*"

She sighs. "Look. I don't actually know how much of a chance there is that we're going to find Julianna Farnetti. But I did know that if I put you and Trevor Collins together in a car for long enough, something would happen, and chasing after a ghost was the best way to do it. Probably the only way you'd go along with this."

"With what?" I ask, a little offended. Julianna Farnetti was the point of the whole trip, in my mind.

"With *this*." Kat gestures around her like I should understand it. "With letting loose and taking off and having one last hurrah with your best friend and the boy you've wanted since seventh grade." She pauses. "I did this for you, P. For us."

It's clear by her voice and the smile on her face that she thinks I should be happy about this. That she thinks she's doing me a favor. "So, what?" I ask calmly. "All that 'we have to find her,' and 'you're totally right,' was just a bunch of BS?"

When I say the words out loud, I don't bother to hide how mad they make me. I feel stupid, like she's been laughing at me the entire time. Probably with Trevor. Does he think the same thing? Is he just along for the ride and an easy hookup?

"It wasn't *total* BS," Kat says. "It's a crazy idea, and it would be amazing if it actually worked out like that." She pauses and looks at me with what feels almost like pity. "But honestly? I think Julianna Farnetti's at the bottom of Summit Lake with Shane Cruz, and all of this—the journal, and Josh, and the painting—it's pretty impossible."

Her words sting, and the way she just dismisses the entire reason I've risked this trip feels like a slap in the face. I avoid her eyes and focus on the rack of gum behind her because I don't want to look at her right now. "Why would you even *bother* then? What's the point?"

"I'm trying to *tell* you what the point is." Her voice comes out a touch sharper than when she spoke before, but she reels it back in with her next sentence. Her voice is softer.

"This is our last chance for something like this, P, and you never would've done it without her as a reason." She pauses. "Right?"

It's true, but I don't answer her.

"And I would've done it for any reason you gave me—you know why?"

I sigh, not wanting to hear her carpe diem speech right now.

"Because school's about to end, Parker, and when it does, everything's gonna change. You're going away, and I'm staying in town, and no matter how much we want things to stay the same between us, they won't. You'll make a bunch of friends at Stanford who are all crazy smart and driven like you, and I'll stay home and try not to become my mom, and pretty soon there'll be too much between us that's different. Things change, Parker. It doesn't take a valedictorian to figure that out."

She stops and I glance up in time to see her drop her eyes to the floor.

The anger welled up in my chest softens, then starts to recede with the realization that this may be the first time I've ever seen a weak spot in Kat's bravado. She clenches her jaw tight, like she knows she gave too much away. Like she doesn't know what else to say. Kat doesn't do tender moments.

It makes me want to reach out and hug her and promise that none of that is true. But what if it is? What if she's right, and everything changes as soon as I leave? I don't know what to do with this moment either, because now we're both standing awkwardly in the middle of the Casa Junction food mart, and I'm pretty sure if we look at each other, one or both of us is gonna cry.

Then, just like she's always done, Kat steps up when I can't. "I'm sorry," she says, and she puts her hand on my arm, and steps close, forcing me to look her in the eye. "I just wanted us to have one last, big thing together that we'll always be able to look back on and say 'we did that.' And if we find Julianna Farnetti while we're doing it, and you get your happy ending, that's bonus. *And . . .*"

I see a smile creep back onto her face, and I know whatever she's about to say is going to lighten the mood. I'm grateful for it, because I don't want us to be mad at each other anymore. "And what?" I ask.

"And I thought if I could get you and Trevor together, maybe you'd have one more reason to come back after you leave." She shrugs. "Absence makes the heart grow fonder, and all that crap."

It's so ridiculous, I can't not laugh. "Seriously? That's how Trevor fits into all of this? As bait to get me to come home? That doesn't make any logical sense."

She shrugs. "If you'd just give up the whole prim and proper thing, you'd realize he might actually be something worth coming back for. And then you can look back and say *you* did that."

"Oh my God. I'm *not* gonna sleep with him, if that's what you're talking about."

"Sleep with who?" a familiar voice cuts in.

*Of course. Of course he would walk in right at this moment.* The last thing in the world I want to do is turn around with my cheeks on fire, but I force myself. "No one," I manage, and then I pretend to be choosing between a Twix and Sour Patch Kids.

"You. She means she's not sharing a hotel room with you," Kat says, like it's nothing.

"Damn," Trevor says with a smile. "Had I known that was even a possibility I would've gotten my butt in here a lot quicker and made a better case than you just did."

Kat laughs.

I cringe. "It wasn't ever—it's not—what kind of candy did you want again?"

He holds up a pack of Starburst. "Don't worry about it, I got it. You guys ready to get back to the open road and the chance at something worth coming back for?"

I shake my head and make a run for the counter—no strutting this time. Kat laughs again as she and Trevor follow me, and I make up my mind to try not to be mad at her for using my own ridiculous idea to sucker me into this trip. But just because I don't want to be mad doesn't mean I'm not disappointed that she doesn't seem to think there's even a chance. Half of me wonders if it's the same with Trevor, but the other half of me doesn't want to know. I'd rather spend this trip thinking he believes in something impossible too.

When we get back to the car, I claim tired and volunteer to take the backseat. I don't think the blush is ever going to leave my cheeks, and between my outfit and Trevor walking in at the perfect moment for my mortification yet again, I don't feel like riding shotgun. And also—what Kat said to me in the store has left me with this sad, uneasy feeling I need to sort out.

Of course things change, that's a given. I've spent the last four years of my life working and waiting for them to change. Always waiting for the next thing—to graduate, to leave town, to go to college. And it's felt like an eternity. Time goes by slowly when you spend it waiting. But now, all of a sudden, it feels like everything has sped up. Or like it's actually been flying by this whole time, and I've been too busy waiting to see what was happening all around me. Now I don't know if it's too late to try.

## 24.

### "One Step Backward Taken"
#### —1945

Three hours, two pit stops, and a carful of empty candy wrappers later, we pass a highway sign that reads HARMONY 5 MI, and a tremor that's a mix of nervous anticipation and all the junk I've eaten passes through my stomach.

"We made it!" Kat cheers from the front. She looks back at me, probably expecting me to match her enthusiasm, but I'm too busy freaking out inside. We really did make it. We're here. In Harmony. The town where Julianna Farnetti might be after all these years.

"You want me to go straight to the gallery?" Trevor asks over his shoulder.

*I want to puke, actually.* I don't know what's worse—the

possibility that she might be there or the possibility that I'm wrong about this whole thing. I look out the window at the rolling green hills, try to follow their graceful curves to calm the storm thundering around in my chest. Then I stall.

"Maybe we should get something to eat first—and make a plan. Aren't you hungry again by now, Kat?"

"Surprisingly, no. Weird, huh? It might be because I burned all of my taste buds off with too much sour crap. So it's your lucky day—we can go straight there."

I look to Trevor like he can help me. "What about you? Did you want to have lunch or something? The beach is over those hills, just a few miles away. We could go there first, and then come back in a little while." It's more of a plea than a suggestion.

"Nah, I'm good," he answers. Our eyes meet in the rear-view mirror. "I think we should go to the gallery. It's kinda what we just drove four hundred miles for. You'll be fine."

*Fine? Really, are you kidding me?* He glances back at me one more time, waiting for a response. Maybe it's from so many years of practice saying one thing while thinking another, or maybe it's because his voice actually does sound reassuring, but after a long moment, I nod. "Okay. You're right. Let's just go and get it over with."

"Wait. Did you just say get it *over* with?" Kat asks from the front seat. She turns around now so we're face to face. "Parker, you have to stop thinking of things that way. Whatever happens, this is a big fucking moment for you. Don't you dare just 'get it over with.' Go in there and *do* something with it. Carpe fuckin' diem." I wince a little at her trucker mouth. She sits back in her seat and faces forward like that's all there is to it, case closed, which gets a surprised laugh from Trevor.

"Wow." He looks at me in the rearview again. "I think she just wrote your speech for you, Frost."

"Yes. My God, yes. Concise, eloquent, *and* inspired." I say it with a smile, but the reminder about my speech sends another wave of nausea through my stomach. I wonder if my mom has read it yet, the one I left for her, that I didn't write at all.

Kat shrugs. "Some things need to be said. And sometimes they require strong words." For Kat, this is true. The real measure of how passionate she is about something is whether she invokes an f-bomb. "Anyway, what I was trying to say is that it's now or never."

And at that moment it is. In the flurry of Kat's inspirational speech I'd barely registered the few galleries we'd driven past that made up the whole of Harmony. We pull over at the curb in front of the last one on the street— a tiny, weather-worn building with a hand-painted sign swaying gently in the breeze. It's a deep blue that matches the trim, and there are no words on it. Just the triple spiral symbol that makes my breath catch when I see it

"Pretty sure this is it," Trevor says, switching off the ignition. In the quiet that follows, the bigness of the moment fans out and seeps into all three of us. We don't say anything, but peer out the car windows at the building in front of us. It's not a fancy art gallery, by any means. It looks more like an old beach cottage than anything else, almost out of place against the hills dotted with cows and wildflowers. There's one big window in the front, but the sun reflects off it at just the right angle to make it near-impossible to see through to the inside.

"I can't even tell if it's open," I say in a renewed effort to stall. "It doesn't look like anybody's here."

"Only one way to find out," Kat says. She swings her door open dramatically and hops onto the sidewalk, taking a moment to stretch in a way that makes her look like an ad for just how sexy rumpled clothes and long, unruly road-trip hair can be.

I gulp and grab the journal like it's a life preserver. Or maybe something more—like it's proof that I have a reason to be here at this place, about to bring up a past that has been long buried.

Trevor gets out at the same time as me, and when our eyes meet he gives me a nod and quick smile of encouragement. "Carpe diem, right?"

"Right."

"You know what you're going to say yet?"

I shake my head. "No idea."

"Doesn't matter," Trevor answers. "If you see her you will. You'll say the truest thing you know and that'll be exactly right."

I look at him with his wrinkled shorts and morning messy hair, and I swear I fall in love right there. I am in love with what he just said. In that moment, no one could have said anything more right or perfect to me. I could . . . I could kiss him right there—

"There's a girl in there," Kat calls over her shoulder and

across the hood of the Jeep. "And she's blond." She crouches down, like we're busted if the girl sees us.

Trevor and I steal a glance at each other again, and the now familiar zing runs the entire length of my body. I'm not sure whether it's my newfound, unabashed desire to kiss him or the fact that Julianna Farnetti could be standing just feet away from us, but I step forward confidently and Trevor falls in right beside me. When we meet Kat on the sidewalk, she does too, and the three of us stride up to the front door of the gallery as one, hopeful, united front.

There's a soft tinkling of wind chimes that hang from the door when I open it. The air inside is soft with the scent of something delicate and floral. It's exactly what I would imagine her choosing. Whoever Kat saw from outside must've stepped through the door I can see at the rear of the room, because the space is empty but for the paintings on the walls and the lazy tendril of smoke rising from a candle on the counter.

"Hi! Come on in!" A bright voice calls from beyond the doorway. "I'll be right there!"

The three of us look at each other. Ask the silent question we're all thinking: *Is it her?* Kat yells back, "Thank you! We'll just take a look around!" in a voice far more chipper and cheery than she'd ever use in real life. I give her a look. She gives me one back and walks over to a stormy seascape on the wall, hands behind her back like a practiced art peruser. Trevor takes a cue from her and does the same with another painting—this one of a solitary oak against a sapphire sky. I stand in the middle of the gallery, hugging the journal to my chest and waiting. Waiting for a ghost to walk through the door in front of me.

But what comes through the door a few seconds later is not a ghost at all. She's more like . . . a Barbie. "Hiiiii-eeee!" She says it like it's two words, and with a startling amount of enthusiasm after that much tension and anticipation. "Welcome you guys! How *are* you today?" All of this comes out in quick succession from her perfectly glossed lips and twinkly white smile. She's tiny, blond, like Kat had said, and is wearing a long dress that manages to look hippyish and expensive at the same time. She's Boho Barbie.

"Hiii-eee," Kat imitates. "We're *great*, thank you. *Love* these paintings. Are you the artist?" She glances at me for a quick second, and we wait for an answer.

The girl blinks then laughs. Even her laugh is sparkly. "Me?" She lays a perfectly manicured hand on her chest. "Oh God, no, I *wish*! I don't actually *do* art. I just like to be around it." I breathe a sigh of relief at this. There's still a chance. I'm about to ask who the artist is, but the girl goes on. "And I'm actually pretty good at selling it, which is why Hope hired me. She doesn't like to deal with that part of it. Kind of a free spirit, artistic thing or whatever, so I work the gallery and she travels and paints and chases her music."

"You mean muse?" I can't help myself.

"Yeah, muse. Anyway, my name's Ashley and I can help you with anything you need."

While Trevor seems amused and content with observing, I can tell Kat's about to have a field day with this girl, so I jump in. "Is there any chance she'll be in today? Hope?

We've come a long way and I really need to talk to her about something important."

"Maybe?" Ashley shrugs. "She's leaving tomorrow for some island I've never heard of and won't be back for a month. But she said she was going to try and bring a few more paintings in before she leaves. Like I said, she has that whole free spirit thing going on—which my parents would think is totally ridiculous, but I totally admire. You don't see that very much where I'm from, you know?"

"And where are you from?" Kat asks. I can hear the subtle sarcasm in the question, but it doesn't seem Ashley can.

"Orange County," she says simply. "Newport Beach."

Kat laughs. "Really? I never would have guessed. You seem so down to earth."

I shoot Kat a look that I'm hoping says, *Get over yourself and be nice. We need her help.*

"Really?" Ashley squeals. "Thank you! I've really been trying to tone down the whole OC thing. You know, live a simpler life. It's why I came up here. Well, that and we have a vacation house I've been staying at over in Cayucos."

"That's really great," I say, making sure to sound nicer than Kat did. I need to get us back on track, especially with "Hope" skipping town tomorrow. "So, Ashley, is there any way you could *call* Hope? I'm only in town for today, and since she's leaving tomorrow, it would be my only chance to talk to her and it's *really* important. Like, life-changing important." I look her in the eye and plead as best I can with my own.

"Life-changing? Are you sure?" Ashley asks. She sighs.

Looks concerned. "I don't know. She's super busy getting ready to leave, and . . . she doesn't really like surprises. She mostly keeps to herself." She pauses and bites her lip. "But if it matters that much, maybe I could let her know what it is that's so important. And then she can decide."

I get the feeling that Ashley genuinely likes to help people, and that she's right on the edge of going out on a limb for me.

"Okay, um . . . can you just tell her it's about Orion?" I say. And I surprise myself when I do. It's a risky move, to leave her the name that's bound to bring up exactly what she's been hiding from for so long, if it really is Julianna. But I'm almost positive that if it's her, his name will be the one thing that might get us a phone call back. Ashley looks confused. "She'll know what it means," I say.

"Okaaay . . . that's weird, but I'll tell her if she comes in or calls. Did you want to leave a number?"

"Yes. Please." I open the journal and start to tear a blank page from the back, and for a second I regret it. If "Hope" really is Julianna, and I do get a chance to give her the journal back, maybe she'll want to fill the remaining pages with the rest of the story.

Ashley goes behind the small counter and grabs a pen for me and I write down my name and cell phone number with a shaky hand, then slide it across the glass to her. "Thank you. I can't really say any more. But you seem like someone who cares about her and this is really important. So please, please have her call me if you can. Or even just give me a call if she comes in and I'll come right back."

Ashley looks at me with serious eyes that soften when she smiles. "No problem," she says. "It's what I do."

"Thank you. Thank you so much."

She tucks my number in her pocket. "You're welcome! Anything else you guys need? Restaurant recommendations, hotels, things to do while you're in town?"

"Yes, all of that, actually," Kat says. "Somewhere to eat lunch would be good."

We leave twenty minutes later after a detailed discussion of hotels and restaurants, all in the next town over, but as soon as we walk out the door I turn to Kat and Trevor. "You guys, I know it's her. It has to be her. Did you hear what she said about Hope keeping to herself? Of course she does. She's been hiding all these years." I pause a moment, struck by the sad similarities of Julianna's and Orion's lives. It makes me more sure than ever that their paths are supposed to cross again, and they're not supposed to continue on by themselves, regretting what might have been.

"I'm not going anywhere," I say, planting my feet. "I'm staying here all day. She has to come by her own gallery if she's planning on leaving town tomorrow."

Kat looks up and down the empty road. There are three buildings on each side, and a barn-looking type thing at the end. "P, there's nothing here. And the beach is *right* over those hills, you said yourself. And little miss friendly in there said she'd call if she comes in. Let's just go to the beach for a little while and we'll come back, I promise. I didn't come all this way to sit in a town—which, by the way, makes ours look like a city—waiting for a girl who may or may not be Julianna Farnetti."

Anger flares up in me fast, and I surprise myself by stepping right up to Kat, close. "And I didn't come all this way to miss Julianna Farnetti by one day, Kat. *Seriously*. How can you even *think* of leaving when we're this close?"

"How can *you* think of sitting here wasting a day waiting around for someone who might not be the right person to maybe stop by?" Kat folds her arms over her chest and glances over the hills separating us from the beach she so desperately wants to see, and like that, she looks selfish to me. I don't understand what's going on with her. Why she's so hot and cold and all over the place with me and this whole thing.

Frustration puts a sharp edge in my voice. "All the more reason to stay here in case she *does* come."

Trevor cuts in, his tone obviously meant to keep the peace. "Hey, I have an idea. Kat, if you want, you can take my car over to the beach for a little while and Parker and I will stay here and watch the gallery in case the mystery girl stops by." He pauses and looks at each of us encouragingly. "Is that good with everyone?"

Kat looks from him to me and back again. "Perfect," she says.

Trevor hands over his keys without hesitating. "Just go easy on her, okay?"

She smiles. "Of course." And just like that our roads diverge.

## 25.

"Something there is that doesn't love a wall,
That wants it down."
—*"MENDING WALL"*

My road doesn't go very far. Trevor and I find a bench two doors down from the gallery, and plant ourselves on its peeling white paint. I shiver a little when the backs of my legs touch the cool of the bench, and wish I would've thought to grab my sweatshirt out of the car before Kat drove off with it on her solo adventure. But it all happened so fast, I wasn't really thinking. I was more just in shock that she left. I still can't believe she ditched us in the middle of our trip, in what I'm not even sure qualifies as a town. I look down the road past the last building on the street, which isn't very far, but she's long gone. The only things there are the fluffy white clouds gathering on the horizon for what looks like an afternoon thunderstorm. Perfect. I let out a heavy sigh, and sit back against the crackly paint curls.

Trevor turns to me. "You wanna talk about it?"

"About what?"

"About whatever's bugging you. Kat, that journal, this trip . . ."

"No. Thank you."

"All right," he says. He sits back next to me like he's ready to settle in and get comfortable, which strikes me as funny since this bench is about the furthest thing from comfortable I can imagine.

I set the journal down and tuck my legs up under me. "Thank you for sticking around. You didn't have to. Kat's probably more fun right now."

"I'm good here," he says, and he leans his head back on the bench.

We're quiet, which I guess is my fault since I said I didn't want to talk about anything, but now the silence feels too heavy, and actually, I do want to talk about it, because I have no idea what just happened with Kat.

"I don't understand what her problem is, you know?" I say it more to the sky than to Trevor. "One second she wants me to 'take chances,' and 'go on adventures,' and 'seize the day,'"—I notch angry air quotes around each of the phrases—"and when I finally decide to, she could care less. She'd rather go spend the day at the beach. What the hell?" I stand up and kick a rock without taking my eyes off the gallery, just in case. I shake my head and sit back down. "I can't figure her out right now."

"She's scared," Trevor says, matter-of-factly.

I scoff. "Kat's never been afraid of anything in her life."

"Yeah, I think that's kind of a front." He peels a curl of paint from the bench and flicks it.

"What do you mean?"

He shrugs. "Back at the rest stop, when you guys were fighting. You sounded mad, but she sounded worried."

"You heard that whole thing?" I reach back for what exactly we said, and hope at the same time, it wasn't too much.

"Not the whole thing," he says. "Just the tail end of it." A little smile tugs at the corners of his mouth, and he looks away. We fall quiet again, and now I'm sure he heard the whole thing.

"I get it," he says. "Why she's worried. You guys are like a team. The only thing she ever talks to me about is you."

A heavy dose of guilt hits me along with his words. I'm the one breaking up the team by leaving. "So what am I supposed to do? Not go? I can't stay at home. I'm done there. And she won't come with me, I've tried."

Trevor thinks about it a moment, and though I'm determined not to take my eyes off the gallery, they drift back to his and watch as they run over the endless green hills in the distance. It startles me when they meet mine as he speaks.

"Maybe just . . . tell her that. Before it's too late and you guys misunderstand each other and make all kinds of wrong assumptions like girls always do." That right there catches me. And the way his eyes hold mine when he says it. I swear they flash with some sort of double meaning, like Kat's not the only thing he's talking about.

"I bet she'll come around if you do," he adds. "Just tell her, straight out . . . how you feel." He doesn't look away, and neither do I, and all of a sudden I'm positive we're not talking about Kat anymore.

"Oh, yeah? You have a lot of experience with that? Being straightforward?"

He grins. "I haven't been anything *but* with you for the last six years."

I nearly choke on the laugh that rises, sudden and nervous, in my throat. We've always walked the line between being genuine and joking, and right now I can't tell which side of it he's on. I decide to bring us back to joking, where it's safe. "*Really?* So had I ever taken you up on the art closet thing, it would've lasted less than four minutes?"

Now he laughs. "No. That was just an appeal to your practical, nonditching ways. I'd take my time with you. I *have* taken my time with you."

I open my mouth but no words come out. No joke or sarcastic remark. He's stunned me silent, and what makes it worse is that though I can feel how ridiculous I must look with my mouth hanging wide open like that, I can't seem to close it. *He's taken his time?* Flirting and joking around for six years could qualify, I guess. But still. He's had plenty of girls to keep him busy in the meantime. He hasn't exactly waited around for me.

I'm about to say so, but I think better of it. And then because I'm feeling brave, but not brave enough to make a real first move, I keep my eyes on his and say, "I wish every-one would say how they really feel. In plain words."

I throw it out like a challenge. An invitation to cross the line, like Julianna had said, between something and nothing, or before and after. And then I panic inside, but I don't look away, and neither does Trevor, and I know we're *right* there. So close it would only take a second to close up the space between us and tell him how I really feel without needing any words at all. I want to lean in and just kiss him like I didn't do that day in my car. Kiss him like I've been telling myself I didn't want to for just as long as he's maybe been waiting for me to do it. I swear he's thinking the same thing, because the air between us is charged with more than just the hint of a storm.

A smile breaks over his lips, and he looks down at his lap, almost laughing to himself.

"*What?*" I snap out of it, feeling fluttery and defensive. He shakes his head, laughs some more. "Oh my God, *what?* What did I say that's so funny?"

Trevor gets a hold of himself. "Nothing, just the straight-forward thing." He smiles. "You should try it some time— being honest about what *you* want." His eyes run over me, searching for a reaction. "Or maybe you're still not sure."

Indignation drops my jaw this time. I want to come back with something—an argument, a joke, a pointed comment about how maybe he's not sure either because he could've kissed me just as easily. What *is* it with him?

Trevor stands slowly, and in that motion, heads off any response from me. "Anyway . . . you wanna get some ice cream? I think it might be the only thing they sell to eat in this town."

"No. Thanks." I shake my head and focus all of my attention on the door of the gallery.

He glances over at it, then back to me. "Finding her means a lot to you, huh?"

I look at the journal in my lap, fight the urge to trace her name with my fingers. "Yeah. I don't know why. It probably seems stupid to even hope."

"No, it doesn't," Trevor says. He shoves his hands in his pockets. "It'd be like a movie. Like one of those chick flicks. If you find her, it means all those things are out there to believe in—true love, and fate, and all that."

I don't know what to do with this, what he just said. I search his face for any trace of teasing, but there's none. He just looks at me like it's the simplest thing in the world to understand. He put into words something I didn't even know I thought, but as soon as he said it, I knew it couldn't be any more true. That's exactly it. If I could actually find Julianna, and tell her about Orion and the café, and her painting, it would mean something. If I could get her to go back for him, to find him where he went back to find her, it would mean things like that really were possible. True love, meant to be, fate, destiny, serendipity, kismet. They're all big, romantic words. Words saved for movies and books and fiction. Not for real life. In real life parents get divorced, and people live unfulfilled lives, and love goes unrequited, and there are no second chances, or do-overs, or perfect moments.

"Am I wrong?" Trevor asks me.

"No, no . . . I just . . . how did you know that? I don't even think I knew that, but it's true."

He smiles. "I have three older sisters, Frost. I've seen a lot of chick flicks against my will. Everyone wants the people to end up together in the end. It's human nature. The funny thing is, you always know they're going to. You just never know how."

I look down at the journal. "That's the best part. The how."

Again we're quiet, but this time there's no tension. It feels like we've just agreed on something. Trevor looks from me to the gallery and back again. "So how 'bout this?" He reaches down, and I'm surprised when he takes my hand, but I let him pull me up from the bench so we stand facing each other.

"I'm willing to bet that we can walk around this entire town—and not lose sight of that gallery," he says.

I glance over at it, then sweep my eyes up and down the empty street. He's right. And we're holding hands, and his grip is firm, and I don't want to let go. "All right," I say, trying to hide a smile. "Twist my arm."

Instead, he squeezes my hand, and we walk, knowing where we're going, just not sure about how we'll get there.

## 26.

"So all who hide too well away
Must speak and tell us where they are."
—*"REVELATION"*

In the space of an hour we've managed to tour the entire "town" of Harmony without ever taking our eyes off the gallery, and not one person has come in or out of it. After stopping by the old creamery for ice cream, we found a closed saloon, an open wine-tasting room that does, in fact, check IDs, a wedding chapel, and a glass blowing studio full of beautiful, swirled "tobacco" pipes hand blown by an aging hippie who didn't bother to pull his wild gray hair back into a ponytail. Apparently this is one of those places that people only come to for art, drinking, smoking, and getting married.

By the time we finish our lap, the clouds have multiplied

and deepened to an ominous shade of gray. We sit back down on the bench, and the easy talking and laughing of our walk subsides into quiet. I check my phone for the millionth time. No missed calls. Not from my mom, which is a good thing, but not from Kat either, which worries me a little. It's late afternoon now, and I would've thought that even if she were mad at me, she would've called or come back by now.

My hopes lift a bit at the sound of a car coming from the direction of the highway, but when it makes the turn onto the main street, I see it's just a beat-up pickup truck. The truck slows and comes to a stop, and a man and a woman get out and begin unloading the back. They take out one of those fold-up tables and a few chairs, then begin to cover the table with cardboard cases full of oranges and avocados. In the next few minutes several other trucks and cars pull up, all of them setting up makeshift produce stands.

"Guess Harmony has a farmers' market too," I say to Trevor.

He's eyeing a truck that arrived towing a large, half barrel that's now sending wood smoke drifting in our direction. "More importantly, they have barbecue."

We watch as the empty main street of the town becomes an outdoor country market filled with citrus and olive oil, avocados and honey-filled mason jars in flavors like lavender and orange blossom. Other cars begin to pull up, and families with strollers and people toting reusable shopping bags fill the street. A music trio sets up near our bench and a woman wearing a long skirt and Birkenstocks tests the microphone while the two guys who are with her tune their guitars. In no time the ghost town we've spent the afternoon walking around becomes a bustling outdoor market filled with live music, barbecue smoke, and kids running around with painted faces and cotton candy.

"Wow," Trevor says. "Who knew?"

"Really." I scan the crowd, being careful to keep the gallery in my sights. "Where did all these people just come from?"

Trevor shrugs. "There're all kinds of little towns nearby. Maybe this is what they all do on Mondays. Wanna check it out?"

"Sure." I stand, wanting to find a place closer to the gallery now that there are so many people milling around. As we walk, I scan for blond hair and come up with matches in every direction. It makes me nervous as I search each of their faces for some trace of the girl whose journal I'm still holding. I want to think that I would recognize her right away, but the truth is, ten years is a long time, and she could be any one of these people walking around me. She could have a child with her, or be strolling down the street holding hands with a new love. There's nothing that says she'll be alone. Or easy to recognize.

"You wanna stick close to the gallery?" Trevor asks. His eyes run over the people we pass too, and it makes me feel good that both of us are looking for her.

I nod and we duck between two booths selling the same assortment of oranges, lemons, and avocados. It's getting harder to make out people's faces in the dusky light, so camping out in front of the gallery seems the safest bet. We stand in front of the window, hands in our pockets, with nothing else that we can really do except wait.

Inside the gallery a few people mill about, and I see that Ashley has put out wine and a cheese platter. She's standing in front of the ocean painting, having an animated, one-sided conversation with a woman who holds a glass of wine in one hand and a cracker in the other and doesn't seem to be listening.

"Bet she's not there for the art," Trevor says.

I watch Ashley talk as the woman sips. "Bet you're right."

The only other people in the gallery are a middle-aged man—maybe the woman's husband—who is posted up right next to the food, helping himself, and a petite, dark-haired woman in skinny jeans and a lacy tank top, who looks more like she belongs at a tattoo shop than an art gallery. A fat raindrop lands on the back of my hand, and then another hits my cheek. Out of the corner of my eye, I see Trevor flinch, then wipe a drop from his forehead before we both turn back to the gallery window.

What I witness next happens in quick succession and in slow motion at the same time. I see Ashley say something to the one in the tank top, who then walks over and shakes the hand of the woman holding the wine glass. Ashley talks between them, gesturing at the ocean painting, and the wine woman brings her free hand to her chest in an emphatic gesture. The brunette nods graciously and tries to inch away, but then Ashley stops her and ushers her over to the glass counter. She looks confused at first, but Ashley picks up a slip of paper and hands it to her. As soon as she reads what it says, the confusion on her face tumbles into something else. Something like fear and recognition, and at that instant, that is exactly what I feel.

She's visibly shaken. The paper slips from her fingers and flutters to the floor. I suck in a deep breath. My phone buzzes in my pocket. Trevor looks from me to the girl falling apart in the gallery. A raindrop lands in my eye, blurring my vision momentarily. I'm suspended in the moment, paralyzed.

Trevor's voice cuts through it and his hand grabs the phone from mine. "It's Kat. I'll talk to her. You go. Now. That has to be her."

I look from him back to the gallery, and Ashley and the couple are still there, and Ashley looks like she's apologizing or something, and the girl—Julianna—is gone. I burst through the door, a rush of wind and rain and desperation and hope.

Ashley looks at me, startled. "Oh—um, she just left. I'm so sorry, I—"

"Where did she go?"

"I don't know, I—"

I don't wait for her to finish. I push past the three of them and duck through the doorway I saw Ashley come out of earlier. It's a small hallway with a door on each side and one in front of me that didn't close all the way. Rain and mist sneak through the crack, and I know she went out that door.

Raindrops prick my face with cold when I step outside again. I look around, desperate. She can't have disappeared into thin air. To the left there's nothing but emptiness. The dark backs of buildings, and a few trash cans next to their back doors. I look to the right, and just in time, I see her small figure, which looks fragile in the rain, about to turn the corner at the end of the street.

"JULIANNA!"

She freezes, and in the light from the corner building I see her turn, just slightly. Then she grabs the door handle in front of her, yanks it open, and disappears behind it.

I run. Through the rain, past one, two, three buildings and their doors, until I get to the one she went in, and when I burst through that one, it's with little hope that she'll actually be inside. Cigarette smoke and the smell of alcohol rush at me on warm air, and I realize I'm in the saloon that was closed earlier. It's packed now, with every table taken and barely any standing room at the bar. My heart beats a desperate rhythm in my chest. *Be here, be here, be here.* I repeat it like a prayer as I take my first tentative steps through the crowd of people. And then it's answered.

She's there. Sitting at the far end of the bar, forehead resting in one hand so that I can't see her face, but I know it's her. My feet step beneath me, my hand reaches under my shirt for the journal, and I forget to breathe. I forget everything else except for Julianna Farnetti, who lifts her head just as I get to her and looks at me with complete and utter anguish in her green eyes.

I don't have the right words for this moment. But then I do. I have hers. Without saying anything, I walk over to where she's sitting, set her journal on the bar, and slide it over to her.

## 27.

"So dawn goes down to day.
Nothing gold can stay."
—1923

I sit on the small couch in a tiny studio apartment directly above the gallery with the rain pouring down in what seems like a roar compared to the heavy, silent stillness between us inside. I feel like a trespasser, like being here in the tiny space that is obviously hers is an invasion. I try to make myself small, unintimidating, nonthreatening. I don't want her to think I'm here to out her secret or reveal her if she doesn't want to be. The quiet between us feels tenuous, and despite the harshness of her dyed dark hair and the heavy eyeliner that's smudged from the rain, she looks fragile. Like this— me being here—could be enough to break her.

I'm careful with this moment because I want to be careful with her. She moves very deliberately in the small kitchen area—filling a teakettle, setting it on the burner. Avoiding my gaze. I try to reassure her by avoiding hers, too. My eyes trail over the details of her life here—not as Julianna Farnetti, but as Hope, artist who would prefer to remain anonymous. There are canvases in various stages of completion leaned in stacks against the wall facing the couch. An easel. A table near the window, and on it, a single white flower in a cobalt glass vase. On the nightstand next to the bed is a white candle burned down low, and a sketchbook. All objects that add up to a simple life.

From what I can see, it's also a lonely life. There are no pictures in frames, no postcards on the refrigerator. No evidence that her existence here and now is anything but solitary. I think of Orion in his café, alone, hiding behind walls of work and art, and it strikes me—the sad, poetic kind of symmetry of each of them without the other. The thought of it is enough to give me the resolve not to leave here without trying to set it right. Because I feel like I'm seeing one of the most tragic things in the world—when two people step away from the paths they're traveling, and those paths go on to cross later, without them. They crossed again the day I found her journal, leaving me as the point of intersection, and I made a choice to try and bring them back together.

The whistle of the teakettle draws my eyes back to the kitchen where Julianna sets two mugs on the counter and pours steaming water into them. She drops a tea bag into each one, and pauses a moment before picking them up.

Then she squares her small shoulders, carries both mugs to the sofa where I'm sitting, and sits opposite me, one leg folded beneath her.

I should say something, I know, but I have no voice. We pick up our cups, quiet, like we're both trying to find the words to begin. Watching each other. She's not anything like how I pictured, but she's stunning just the same. Her high cheekbones are more apparent, the green of her eyes deeper than any of the pictures I've seen. Her hair is damp from the rain and hangs wavy and dark over her slight shoulders, which makes the streak of blond in the front leap out. In the open V of her tank top I can see a delicate, necklacelike tattoo over her collarbone. She reaches up to tuck the blond behind her ear with a ringed hand, and I catch a glimpse of a tiny bird inked onto her wrist. It reminds me of Orion with all of his tattoos, and I wonder if maybe they both found some sense of solace in having them done—another parallel they don't even know about.

I take a sip from my cup and glance at her journal sitting on the coffee table between us. When we'd come into her apartment, she'd set it there and retreated to the kitchen like it was something that could hurt her, which I suppose it is. There's so much contained in its pages. A whole life she disappeared from. The girl she used to be. A love she left behind. She looks at it now too, and though there are so many things I want to ask her, this moment feels fragile, and so I choose my words carefully.

I clear my throat. "It was in a box I was going through for Mr. Kinney. His senior journal project from ten years ago.

From your class. I'm his TA. I was getting them ready to send out." I take a deep breath and look down into my tea, dreading what I have to say next. "When I got to your name, I was . . . I didn't know where to send it, and . . ."

In all the times I'd thought of finding her, I'd never anticipated how excruciatingly hard it would be to confess that I'd read her journal—words that were supposed to be hers alone, not meant for anyone else to see. It felt like a terrible trespass at the time, but now it feels far, far worse. Like something that can't ever be taken back, or forgiven even.

The silence stretches tight between us, and I can feel her waiting for me to break it. "Um, I took it. And then . . ." The three words are heavy in my chest, and I have to force them out. "I read it."

She takes a breath now, the kind you take in to keep from crying out when something hurts. The sound of it sends guilt coursing through every inch of me.

"I'm so sorry," I say, looking down. "I never thought there was any possibility that you could still be . . . that you were even alive. I mean, there's a billboard at the edge of town with your picture on it, and a memorial at Summit Lake, and there's a scholarship at school that I was supposed to write a speech for, and . . ." I shake my head. "I know I shouldn't have read it."

I look back up at her, pleading with my eyes, and try to make her understand with my words. "I was seven when you disappeared, and I remember it like my grandma remembers when JFK got shot, or the way my parents remember that space shuttle exploding. Just like that, I remember how you disappeared, and how everyone went out into the storm looking for you. The whole town remembers."

I pause, hoping my words aren't making her feel guilty. I'm trying to keep myself from feeling guilty. "And so when I found your journal, with your words in it, I read it." I pause and chance a look at Julianna. "I wanted to know who you really were."

She laughs in a forced way that doesn't have a trace of happiness to it. "*I* didn't know who I was then. When I was writing all of that." She looks at the journal like she remembers exactly what's in it. It's the first time I've heard her voice, and it's so full of sadness I feel a lump in my own throat.

I swallow hard over it. "It seemed like you were just finding out," I say, timidly. She nods, but I can tell she's far away right then. Back there, maybe. Maybe thinking about Orion, wondering how it could've been different. I want so badly to tell her everything, all in one breath, but I hold it back. It seems important that I let her lead.

Finally, after what seems like forever, she speaks again. This time, she tries to keep her voice calm, but her eyes are full of fear. "How did you find me?"

This is the big moment. This is exactly the question I want to answer, because it's why I'm here. Orion is why I'm here. The two of them being brought back together is why I'm here.

"Your painting," I say. "*Acquainted with the Night*. It's hanging on the wall of a café back home." Her eyebrows rise in surprise. I nod. "I know. It seems crazy. That one of your paintings somehow ended up back there." If she thinks it is, she doesn't say so. And I realize, as I'm about to go on, that

that's not nearly the craziest thing I'm going to tell her.

"I recognized the spiral of the signature from the pages of your journal. You started putting it on them after . . ." We both glance at the composition book on the coffee table and she nods like she knows what I mean without me having to say it. She raises her cup to her lips, and I take a chance. I say it anyway. "After the day you wrote about Orion's tattoo."

She freezes at the sound of his name, and I can't tiptoe around it anymore. I clear my throat. Again.

"It's his café that your painting is hanging in. His café called Kismet, which is so perfect because it means fated. And he doesn't even know. He has no idea it's yours, but I saw it, and I knew." The words spill out fast, landing haphazardly. Julianna's not looking at me anymore. I keep going.

"He doesn't go by Orion anymore, and he barely talks to anyone. He's been there ever since you—since you disappeared. But he's kind of a ghost, too. He came back to help look for you, and he's been there ever since, and after I read your journal and figured out he was who he was, I asked him about you." Now she looks at me, and when she does, I see something in her eyes besides sadness and regret. She's gone white, and the teacup, still at her lips, begins to tremble.

I reach out and take it gently from her. Her hands fall to her lap, but she keeps her eyes on mine. "He doesn't know," I say quickly. "He doesn't know you're here, or that I came to find you, or any of it. I didn't want to get his hopes up until I knew for sure because—" I stop, realizing that I was wrong seconds ago, thinking it was the big moment. It's now. It's what I'm about to say.

"Because?" she whispers.

"Because he still loves you. He's never gotten over you. He went back hoping to find you, and he's been there ever since, and he's sad. He's alone, and sad, because he's loved a ghost for the last ten years."

She lets out a breath and looks down at her hands in her lap. They're paint speckled, just like she wrote about his being, and I want to point it out to her, how perfect that one thing is. She's crying now, and I'm sure they're happy tears, because after what she wrote, and after finding her living the same kind of sad, lonely life, she has a second chance. I've just handed it to her.

"It's why I came," I say. "So you would know, and you could come back, and the two of you can be together, because you're supposed to be. There's no other reason why it would've worked out like this. There are so many pieces that came together just perfectly, and I didn't think these things actually happened in real life, but they do, and I found you, and now you can go back."

I stop, out of breath.

And here we are, in the moment I've pictured since I saw the painting and realized it was hers. This is where she jumps up, tears of joy streaking her face, and says "Let's go back." This is where we leave her apartment without bothering to turn the lights off or blow out the candle because she can only think of getting back to Orion. And this is where we drive through the night and the rain, and we end up in Summit Lakes just as the sun is rising over the razor peaks, splashing warmth and rosy light into the cold granite. This is where the background music rises and swells and we get to Kismet just as Orion is unlocking the door. And he sees her. And she sees him. And it's perfect. I'm so happy, and so caught up in imagining it all that it takes me a moment to notice.

Julianna's shoulders are shaking, and the tears that are now rolling down her face don't look like happy tears. As soon as she brings her green eyes to mine, I see hurt, maybe even anger.

The picture in my mind breaks apart and clatters to the floor of her lonely apartment. "You never should have come here," she says through tears.

I don't believe her. And it makes me want to cry because I don't understand. I don't understand at all. I try to explain it better. Maybe I got too carried away. "Of course I should've come. Don't you *see*? The two of you had something—had that thing that everyone hopes for, and then you lost it, but now you have another chance, and . . ." It's not working, I can tell, but I keep going, pleading now. "You can go *back*, and he'll be there, and I know he'll still feel the same way about you, I know it. It's not too late. It can still be . . ."

I can tell by the look on her face she doesn't think so. I don't finish, and we fall silent. Even the rain outside fades into the silence while I wait for her to say something. And then finally, she does. "I can't ever go back there."

She leans in and takes my hands in hers, looks me in the eye, and speaks forcefully. "And nobody can ever know about me. Especially Orion."

I pull my hands away. "What? *WHY?*" Now I'm angry. "Don't you *see?*"

"Don't *you?*" she fires back at me. "Shane died ten years ago, and it was my fault." She pauses. Makes sure she's still looking me in the eye for what's next. "I ran away," she says. "Like a coward. I let a whole town think I was dead too. There's no coming back from that."

I don't say anything. It'd been there, in me, this worry about what had happened to Shane. First I'd hoped that he had made it out too somehow, that maybe they'd agreed to go their separate ways, start new lives, fresh. But really, I knew that didn't make any sense. I knew there was probably something else, and I'd pushed that thought away. I'd wanted to find Julianna more than anything, but I wanted to find her as I thought of her before. A perfect, beautiful mystery. And I thought I wanted to know what really happened that night. But now, the way she's looking at me, I know I don't. I don't want her to tell me the rest, because I want her to be innocent.

I want her to stay golden.

28.

"Sudden and swift and light as that
The ties gave,
And [she] learned of finalities
Besides the grave."
—"The Hill Wife," 1916

"We weren't fighting. Not at the party, like the papers said after. And Shane wasn't driving when it happened." She pauses. "I was."

A bubble bursts in my mind—everything I'd assumed— gone. She's just rewritten history for me, and I scramble to keep up and reframe it in my memory.

"He'd been drinking, and I wasn't, so I drove when we left, straight out into that storm. And it was the most scared I'd ever been driving in the snow. It was coming straight at the windshield, so hard and fast that the only things I could see in the headlights were the trails of white stretched out in front of us. I couldn't even see the road."

I nod. I know exactly what she's talking about. My mom avoided driving in storms as much as she could, but the few times we had, the view out the window had reminded me of Star Wars, when they shift into light-speed and all that's visible are the stars stretched out blurry in front of them.

"I should've just driven him home. I tried to. His parents would've let me stay the night in the guest room. I would've gone home in the morning, everything could've been different." As she says it, I wonder how many times she's thought those things. How many times she's thought of all the ways it could've been different. I don't say anything though, and she keeps going.

"I decided that morning, before graduation, that I couldn't go another day without telling him that something had changed with me, and that I didn't know if it was something that could change back." Regret washes over her face as she looks at me. "I loved Shane, more than anything, and we'd daydreamed a future together, and it was a perfect one. One I should've wanted, you know? And then I met Orion, and that daydream seemed so much smaller somehow, and it started to feel like it didn't fit right anymore. Because I fell in love with him, too."

She glances down at her hands again, maybe afraid of what I think, but I'm not judging. I'm just listening. It's strange to actually hear her talk about it all, because in my head it was so much different.

"So I told Shane, once we left the party and we were in the car," she continues. "Not everything. Just that I thought

I might need some time to think, that maybe we needed a break to make sure that we were really what we wanted." Her eyes well up again. "I wasn't trying to hurt him. I was trying to do the right thing after doing the wrong thing with Orion. But I did hurt him. So much.

"He didn't say anything at first. He just went silent, and it scared me because he'd never done that before. We'd had arguments, but this was different. There was only the sound of the wipers going, and the wind all around the car, and him not saying anything. And the only thing I wanted was to take it back. I still would, in a second."

She shifts her weight and unfolds her leg from beneath her, and I wonder if she *had* somehow taken it back, been able to smooth it over, how different her life would be. If Shane really would've been the choice she'd made. I can't see it. Not after knowing what I do about her and Orion.

"After that, he got mad. It was hurt coming out as anger, and I could tell it was a bad idea to try and talk about it with him so upset. I tried to take him home, but he kept telling me to just drive. That we couldn't go back until we figured things out. And I was crying, and driving, and he kept asking me what I wanted and what I meant, and I couldn't tell him because I was scared of what I might say."

She pauses to wipe away another tear.

"So I said I didn't know, and that made him more angry than anything, because he said he *did* know what he wanted, that he always had, and that it was me. When he said that, I felt like the lowest person in the world. Like I was throwing away everything that meant anything to me. I hit the brakes.

I wasn't thinking, I just wanted to stop and tell him I was wrong, and that I was sorry. That I took it all back. But the back of the car swerved over the ice, and then we were spinning. I panicked. He grabbed the wheel. We couldn't fix it.

"And then we were falling."

She looks at me with somber eyes, and it feels like forever before she speaks again. When she finally does, she says, "I thought I was dead when we finally stopped at the bottom. We'd tumbled down the side of the ravine, and the noise was deafening all the way down. Metal crunching and glass shattering, and me. Screaming. And then finally we were still, and it was so quiet, I thought I had to be dead. The headlights were still on, and down at the bottom where we were, there was no wind. The snow was still falling, but it was just drifting down in the lights, like feathers after a pillow fight. For a few seconds it was the most peace I'd felt in my life. I closed my eyes, accepted that was the end, and almost felt relief."

I picture her there, inside the Jeep on its side at the edge of the river, the canyon lit up glowing and white with their headlights, and snow falling silent in the night. Thinking that was it. How horrible.

"But then the cold started to seep in," she says. "It was water, from the river, and it stung enough to wake me up, or bring me back, and when it did, the first thing I did was reach my hand out for Shane, but he wasn't there. He wasn't in the car anymore.

"I panicked all over again. I fought with my seat belt, and when I got it open, I climbed out his window. It was broken, and it cut my hands when I did." She shows me the palms of her hands, both crisscrossed with deep scars. "I was so numb with cold and shock, I couldn't feel anything, but I knew I needed to find Shane and make sure he was okay."

Her voice hitches and she has to stop there. Tucks both knees to her chest and buries her head in her arms and cries softly. I say nothing, but I see it in my mind: the snow and wind, words she couldn't take back, the bottom of the ravine. The empty Jeep. I wipe at my own eyes, and wait until she lifts her head.

"I found him because of the blood. It was dark on the snow, like someone had spilled paint all over a canvas, and I followed it to the edge of the river. And then I saw him and"—she pauses to take a breath—"he was on the other side, wedged against a tree branch that bent down into the water. It was holding him there, and the river was moving fast around his legs. His arms were just drifting, and he was so white already. I ran in, and I couldn't feel my hands or my feet, but I had to swim because it was deep where he was." She stops, presses her lips together, and I can see she's reliving every moment as she tells it.

"I almost didn't make it to him," she says. "But I reached out for that branch, and it saved me. And then I was there with him. I put my hand on his cheek and called his name. I screamed it. I slapped his face, and then I put my lips to his and they were already ice, but I pushed air into his mouth again and again because I didn't know what else to do. I begged him to wake up, but he didn't, so I held on, and I tried to hold him, too, until someone came for us. But there was nobody. And then the headlights went out, and I was alone in the dark, freezing to death and trying to hold on for us both. And I had to choose."

Her eyes brim again as she brings them to meet mine. "The only thing I wanted to do was go with him. Follow him, into the dark of the water and the night, because I couldn't imagine life without him." She shakes her head. "But I didn't. I swam to the shore."

I'm the one who's crying now, sitting on the couch of her lonely little apartment, with the rain pouring down outside, and the memory of cold and tragedy filling the space inside. I can see it all, how a word, an action, a series of moments can add up to this, and it makes me want to reach a hand out to her because I can also see the guilt in her shoulders, in her eyes, imprinted permanently into every bit of who she is now.

"I killed him," she says after a long moment. "And he died thinking I didn't love him anymore. I killed *us*. Everything we had, and everything we were, was gone. It disappeared when I said those things to him. And when I realized I could never undo it, or make it right, I wanted to disappear too."

She stops, and when she does, I notice the rain outside has subsided. Instead of a steady shower on the roof, there are intermittent drops. The flicker of her candle against the window. A low hum and a moving beam of light from a passing car below. I almost want everything to stop right there. I'm afraid to hear what comes next in her story, because she did. Disappear.

## 29.

"Two souls may be too widely met."
—"A MISSIVE MISSILE," 1934

I can hear her running water in the bathroom as I sit alone on the couch. I watch the shadows of her feet move in the slice of light coming from beneath the door, like if I take my eyes away, she might disappear again. Just vanish into the night like before. She'd have reason to, with what I know now.

I barely spoke in the last hours, and she unraveled it all, detail after painful detail, like I imagined people did in confession if they were really serious about it. And that's what it felt like—a confession. I didn't ask, but I don't think she'd ever said any of it out loud. But she had no choice with me. Her own words, in her journal, had come back to haunt her and brought me along with them.

So she told me everything. She told me that after she'd swum to the shore, she lay there alone until the snow stopped falling and a blanket of white covered the red of the snow all around her. The clouds moved on, and the stars appeared again, just in time to disappear into the pale light of morning. And that's when she crossed the line she could never come back from. She said good-bye. She didn't say any more than that about Shane, but I knew what that meant. The papers said they'd both been swept down into Summit Lake by the rushing cold water of the river, and I know now they were right about him.

She'd walked all the way to the other side of the lake then, bruised and bleeding, in shock and half frozen. A broken person, lost and then found by a carful of college kids on their way back to Southern California from Summit Lakes. They thought she was lost, a runaway, a victim of something horrible. She let them believe it. They tried to take her to a hospital, get her help, call someone she knew. She told them no, that she just needed to get as far away as possible. And that's what they helped her do.

She didn't go into the details of what happened next. Only said that the months that followed were the darkest she'd ever known, but that the longer she stayed away, the harder it was to think about coming back—like watching a door close by inches and millimeters, until finally it's locked and the key is thrown away.

I listened to everything, weighing each of her words, and trying not to think about what they meant. I tried to put myself in the place where she'd been, but I couldn't. It was a place I didn't even want to imagine, and one that I wasn't sure I could ever understand.

When she finished, she said, "I've been alone for a long time, and it's how my life should be. I caused too many people too much pain, and after this long, going back would do it all over again. I told you all of this so you could understand why, even if I wanted to come back, I couldn't." She paused then, and the certainty in her voice seemed to waver. "Even with Orion there. Even if I thought we had a chance."

I wanted to argue with her, despite everything she'd told me, because a little part of me still believed there was a reason for all of this. For everything. And that maybe it was never too late. But her small jaw was set when she spoke again, and she looked me in the eye, and it was with conviction that she said, "I need you to promise to keep this secret."

"I promise," I answered, and I felt sick and empty when I said it. It's a strange, surreal thing to watch an ideal crumble right in front of your eyes, and to know there's absolutely nothing you can do about it.

Julianna comes out of the bathroom now, her hair pulled back and her face washed clean of the rain and tear-smudged eye makeup, but I can see it's the only thing she's washed clean of. Telling me everything didn't absolve her of anything. Didn't change anything.

"You can stay here if you need to," she says. "I can help you find your friends in the morning before I leave. I'm sure they'll be back here looking for you."

I hope so. After Julianna's story I'd tried to call my phone to at least let Trevor and Kat know where I was, and that I was okay, but it just went to voice mail. Now I have no idea where they are or how I'm going to find them, but I can't stay here any longer. Sitting here on the couch in her living room, it's the saddest, loneliest place I've ever been. I'm angry and frustrated and heartbroken, and I want to hate her for it. I want to hate her for not being who I thought she was, and for not doing what I hoped she would, and jumping at the chance to go back to Orion, because I'm more sure now that she loved him, and had things been different, she might have even ended up with him. But I can't. I'm too sad to hate her.

I look at her standing there, resigned to the choices she's made, and I know there's nothing more I can say or do. I'm finished here. "Thank you," I say, standing up. "But I should go." I glance at the journal on the coffee table. It's where it belongs, but I am not.

Julianna doesn't argue, just nods like she understands. "Thank *you* for just listening like you did. I've never told anyone. And I'm sorry. You must think . . ." She shakes her head. "I don't know what you think. I hope you know I would go back and change it all if I could." Her eyes drop to the floor, away from mine. "But life doesn't work like that, and we all have to live with the choices we make."

She walks me to the door, and we say good-bye, and then just like that, it's over. The story ends with the soft click of her lock sliding into place.

"It doesn't have to be that way," I say to the empty hallway. "You called yourself Hope."

## 30.

"Suppose you've no direction in you,
I don't see but you must continue"
—"TO A THINKER," 1936

I step out the back door of the building and into the dark drizzle with no plan or direction or any idea of what comes next. Maybe after hearing everything I should think she's a horrible person who doesn't deserve another chance. Maybe for a lot of people it would be easy to think that, and decide that who she is now is made up of the things she's done. But I can't. I can't draw that line between wrong and right anymore because she exists somewhere in the space between those absolutes.

It's a truth I'd rather not know. The reality of what happened to her and Shane, and what I saw in her when she said she could never go back make me wish I'd never found the journal in the first place. Never thought there was a different version of the story. Never hoped I could have a hand in writing it. But mostly, it makes me wish I'd never let it mean so much to me.

I round the corner, more lost and low than I've ever been, and just beyond the streetlight's reach, standing beneath an awning with his hands in his pockets, is Trevor Collins. Solid, and real, and waiting for me. The sight of him lifts some of the heaviness from my chest, and I take a few tentative steps toward him.

He looks relieved when he sees me. "Parker, hey." With a hand on my shoulder, he ushers me under the awning with him. "I was getting worried. Thought you might've run off and disappeared with that girl." He pauses, and his eyes search mine in the dim light. "Was it her?"

I glance up at the apartment window above the gallery, where drawn curtains hide a lost girl who doesn't want to be found. And now it's my choice. I can let her stay that way, living a life I'd never wish on anyone, or I can change it for her. Against her will.

I don't have to weigh the options long to realize it's not my place. No matter how much I want it to be different. Trevor's eyes trail up to the window too for a second, then he looks back at me. Waits expectantly for an answer.

"It wasn't her," I say, and again, there's that sick, empty feeling. The words taste wrong.

Trevor's face falls. "Oh no."

"I was wrong," I say, "about everything." I lean against the wall, and he does too, shaking his head like he can't believe it. I don't like lying to him, not at all, but I made a promise to Julianna. "That girl *was* the artist of those paintings, but her name is Hope and she had no idea what I was talking about," I continue. "I think she thought I was crazy at first, but then when I had nowhere to go she let me stay for a while." I look down at my hands. Fumble with them like it'll keep me from crying.

Trevor reaches over and lays a warm hand over mine. "I'm sorry. I know how much you wanted to find her."

I try to shrug it off, try to tell myself not to cry about this. Not right now, in front of him. "It's fine," I say, but my voice has that shakiness that comes along with holding back tears, and I'm sure he can tell. "It was a stupid idea anyway," I add. And then I take a deep breath and watch the mist come down in the glow from the streetlamp, and I realize how true it is. Bringing them back together was a ridiculous idea, and a naive thing to hope for, because life doesn't work like that. Julianna had said it herself.

"It wasn't stupid at all," Trevor says. He turns, and I can feel him looking at me. "It was pretty impressive, actually, the way you chased that girl down."

That almost gets a laugh out of me. I turn to him and he looks at me then—really looks at me, in a way that's surprising because it's so serious. "You know what *is* stupid?" he asks, and he pushes off the wall and stands so we're face to face.

"What?"

His eyes run over mine, and for the second time tonight, everything speeds up and slows down in the space of a few seconds. He steps closer. Brings both his hands to my cheeks. Pulls me into him gently. Speaks words I barely hear. "That's it's taken me so long to—"

His lips on mine finish the rest with a kiss that's light and soft, almost a question. Warmth spreads out in me, and I want to answer him and sink into this kiss, and this feeling. I want to forget about everything that Julianna said and lose myself in this moment, with the rain falling soft and the smell of the wet pavement rising all around us, and his hands on my face like it's where they belong. I want to believe in this moment so much.

But I don't. I can't. I can't because of what I know, and what I've seen, and everything it means.

I pull away. Trevor lets go.

He leans back against the wall and avoids my eyes as I search for something to say to explain. A way to tell him how badly I wish things were different, but I know it's too late. The low hum of an engine, distant at first, then all of a sudden close pulls us both out of the heaviness of the moment. Before we can say anything, the Silver Bullet pulls up right in front of us, and Kat jumps out.

"*Wow*. I spent the whole drive back getting ready to apologize for taking off and being gone for so long, but—" She steps past the headlights and stops between us, smiling. "But now I don't feel bad at all. *Actually*, it looks like you guys owe me a big, fat thank you."

When neither one of us say anything, she catches the tension. "Or maybe not."

"Where *were* you?" I ask, needing to change the subject.

"It's a long story." She looks from me to Trevor and back again. "Probably as long as this one right here. Why don't we go get some food and caffeine, and then maybe we can all share. Yes?"

Trevor clears his throat and pushes off the wall without looking at me. "Food sounds good," he says flatly. "Let's get outta here."

Kat holds out his keys, and he takes them and gets in the driver's seat without saying another word. When I go straight for the back door on the passenger side, she follows me, grabs my wrist before I can get in, and gives me a *What happened?* look. I shake my head without answering and open the door.

What happened is I just lost my last chance. And I hate myself for it.

31.

"But I have promises to keep,
And miles to go before I sleep."
— *"STOPPING BY WOODS ON A SNOWY EVENING,"* 1923

We settle ourselves into the red vinyl booth, Trevor on one side, Kat and I on the other, and after ordering a breakfast for dinner, Kat clasps her hands together on the table, leans forward, and says, "Okay, spill it. What happened with the gallery girl? Did she ever come? Was it Julianna?"

The whole thing rushes back at me for the first time since Trevor kissed me. "No," I say. "It wasn't her." I tell her the same lie I told him, and the weight of it drags me even lower than I already feel.

Kat reaches across the table for my hand. "*Shit.* God, I'm really sorry, P. I know how much you were hoping for it."

Her tone is genuine and sympathetic, and I don't say anything because I can feel the tears ready to spring up if I do. Trevor must see it, because he excuses himself to the bathroom, which I appreciate.

Kat sees it too, and once he's gone, she shifts into pep-talk mode. "Hey—maybe they got a chance to work it out on the other side and they're living happily ever after out there somewhere."

I force a smile. "Maybe so."

"What are you gonna do with the journal?" She asks.

"It's gone too," I say. "I lost it when I went chasing after her."

She frowns. "Really? You were guarding that thing with your life. How'd you lose it?"

I shake my head, avoiding her eyes. "I don't know. I just did."

"Huh. That's too bad."

We're quiet a moment, and then Kat squeezes my hand again. "Maybe it's better that way. It's actually kind of fitting. You found it by chance, and now you lost it by chance. Maybe now chance will send it where it should be."

I nod, but can't muster any enthusiasm or response. Who knows what Julianna will do with it. Maybe I should've given it to Josh instead, so at least he'd know she really had fallen in love with him too.

Kat leans her elbows on the sticky table, then thinks better of it and sits back against the booth. "So what else? What happened with you guys to make things so awkward?" She glances over my shoulder and I turn to see Trevor, who's weaving his way back to the table from the bathroom.

Kat gives me a mischievous smile when I turn back

around. "Did you hook up and it was bad or something?"

I sigh. "Bad. I'll tell you later." I try to think of something to change the subject to quickly. "So where did you go, anyway?"

"Don't you worry your pretty little head about that." She smiles.

"About what?" Trevor asks. He slides into the booth and our legs brush, just for a second, his skin against mine, and we both pretend not to notice.

"About her mom and her speech," Kat says without missing a beat. "It's gonna be bad when she gets home."

I chance a look at Trevor. "My mom's a little . . ."

"Crazy," Kat finishes through another mouthful of French toast.

"I was gonna say strict, but that's a better way to put it." I fiddle with my napkin. "This is gonna be a big deal, if she finds out. Especially if she finds out I left her a Googled speech." My mouth goes dry. "Oh my God. I still have to write the real one."

"We should go home then," Trevor says. He looks at his watch, then at me, but only for a moment. "We can make it back by morning if we leave now, and you can get home, pound some caffeine, and get it done. Maybe she won't find out."

Worry over what will be waiting for me at home closes in, and I want to say no, let's not go back. I don't want to face my mom, or my speech, or the scholarship committee. And I don't think I can stand to ever set foot in Kismet again and chance seeing Josh. Not with what I know now.

"He's right," Kat says. "Let's get you home."

jessi kirby

After we pay our check, we point the Silver Bullet north and drive in silence. I lean my head against the passenger window and watch the night go by. The rain is gone, leaving the sky mottled with patches of clouds and darkness peeking through the places where they've broken apart, but I can't see any stars. Sadness creeps in from the edges all around me, and when we pass the last lights of town and begin backtracking over the miles we traveled only hours earlier, it feels like admitting defeat.

Trevor glances over at me, his expression soft in the glow from the dash. "You can go to sleep if you want. I'm fine driving."

"Thanks. But I don't think I could sleep right now."

He nods and is quiet a moment, but surprises me with what he asks next. "So, would it have been worth it if you'd found her?"

I don't answer right away. I want to tell him the whole thing, every last detail about Julianna and what she said, and how it's all even more sad than we knew before we came.

"Maybe not," I say. "Maybe the whole idea of finding her was better than the reality of it would've been anyway." I pause. Think about all the things we hope for and dream about, and how often they turn out to be different from what we thought. Like that kiss, and what I did.

"I don't know about that," Trevor says, his eyes on the road. "I think a lot of things get even better the closer you get to them." He smiles but doesn't look over at me. "And at least you tried, you know? That should count for something."

"It should," I say. "It should count for something."

## 32.

"I have come by the highway home,
And lo, it has ended."
— *"RELUCTANCE," 1915*

After miles and miles of darkness we crest the grade just below town, and the mountain skyline I've known as home all my life rises up in front of us, towering jagged and dark against a pink sunrise sky. In the past the sight of it has always been welcoming, but today it's a sad reminder that I'm back where I began. Just before town we pass the billboard, where a single light still shines down on the smiling pictures of Shane and Julianna, and the sight of it is ironic in the worst possible way. My eyes fill up and I close them, wanting to push away the secret that sits heavy inside me along with the realization that this is it. The end of the road.

My house is the first stop, since it's at the south end of town, and after seeing how many missed calls I had from my mom when Trevor gave me my phone back, I know I need to get home because she knows. Almost as soon as Trevor pulls into my driveway, the front door opens, and my mom steps out, looking haggard in her robe, and I know she didn't sleep. Guilt and fear swirl around in my stomach.

"Good luck," Trevor says, eyeing her nervously.

"Thanks." I watch as she wraps her arms around herself tightly and starts down the steps. "I'll need it." I put my hand on the door handle and take a deep breath. "Thank you . . . for everything," I say, and I wish I could say more, but my mom is making a beeline for my door. "And . . ."

Trevor glances over my shoulder, then back at me. "Sure," he says.

The door opens behind me, and my mom's voice is as cold as the air it rushes in on. "Get out of the car, Parker. Now."

Kat sits up in the backseat at this. "Please, wait. You should know that this was all my idea, the whole thing. I made her take the trip. Please don't blame Parker."

My mom glances at Kat and then Trevor, who's gone silent, but she doesn't respond. She brings her eyes to mine, and in a low, controlled voice says, "*Get* out of the car now. We will talk about this inside."

I do as I'm told, and as I follow her up my front steps I turn just in time to see Trevor backing out of my driveway. Kat's in the front seat now, making a hand signal for me to call her, and he's looking over his shoulder. I don't even get a last look. My mom closes the door behind me before I get the chance.

Once we're inside she stands there a moment without saying anything, letting me anticipate the weight of what's about to come down on me. I brace myself.

"The school called yesterday afternoon," she says, her voice taut. "Said you were part of the group of seniors who decided to ditch school. So I came home from work early. Waited for you to get home. And I called you, left a message. And I waited. And then I called you again. Then I thought maybe you'd gone to Kat's, so I called there, and guess what? Her mom hadn't seen the two of you either. But you already know that."

Her words are sharp and well aimed, and I know better than to interrupt, so I just keep my mouth shut and my head down and let her get it out.

"So I called you again. And again. And still, no answer. I didn't get angry, Parker, I got worried. So then do you know who I called? Your uncle, who got the rest of the department together, and they went out *searching* for you only to find your car in the high school parking lot. That's right. You and Kat and that boy had the Summit Lakes Police Department out looking for you while you were off somewhere—" She doesn't finish, but heaves a sigh of anger and frustration.

My stomach turns. I hadn't counted on having a search party sent out after us. This makes things exponentially worse. I keep my head down, eyes on the floor. "I'm so sorry."

My mom holds up a hand for me not to say anything more. She's not finished. "So now what you're going to do is

251

call your uncle and tell him that you're home, and safe, and that you're very sorry for taking up the department's valuable time by making a foolish choice to run off on some joy ride."

"It wasn't—"

"What were you *thinking*? *Right* before the scholarship dinner? How could you put that at risk? You *know* how fast word travels, and don't you think for a second that the entire town, including the scholarship board, doesn't know you were missing for a day."

She stops for a breath. "It's going to require an explanation. People are going to ask."

I wince. This gets worse every second.

"So right now, what you're going to do is go into your room and practice your speech until it's flawless. Until you can deliver it well enough to make them forget about this whole fiasco. And later, when you can look me in the eye, you're going to tell me what the hell you were doing."

"Mom—"

She puts a hand up again. "Not right now. Go. I didn't give you a choice."

"You've *never* given me a choice." I match her volume and force with the words, and it shocks us both. The few times I've actually been in trouble for something, I've never answered back like that. I've never argued, or tried to defend myself, or justify it, or stand up for a wrong choice I may have made. Ever since I was little, I've said sorry when she told me she was angry, hung my head if she was disappointed, and nodded like I deserved it when she doled out my consequences.

My mom laughs a humorless laugh. "And this situation

right here is exactly why. Look where making your own choice has gotten you today, Parker." She sighs and shakes her head. "I've spent your life trying to teach you about choices. To teach you how to make the right ones instead of romanticizing all of the wrong ones like your father. And right now I'm not so sure I've done a good job. You've been making bad decisions for the last few weeks, right when all your hard work is about to finally pay off."

She pauses to step closer, her voice softening by the tiniest degree. "You are too young to see it, but every choice you make matters. Every choice has the power to affect your life later on in ways you can't go back and change."

Hurt over her words, and anger and disappointment over Julianna all rush at me, springing hot to my face, and I can't contain it any longer.

"You're right, Mom." I spit the words at her. "I'm too young to see anything like that. I can't see that you're not happy with the choices you've made. Or that maybe Dad finally is. I can't see that sometimes the people who deserve choices don't get them, or that sometimes people who get them throw them away. I can't see any of that. Because I'm too young."

I keep my eyes on my mom's, and when she looks away first I know I've wounded her. It's silent. What's left of the air in the room goes icy. "Go up to your room," she says flatly. "We will deal with this after tomorrow." Her voice has lost its bluster, but I haven't.

"Fine. I will. I'll go up to my room and do exactly what I'm supposed to do because that's who I am. I don't get a choice. Instead I have a plan that doesn't even feel like *mine* anymore. Who needs a choice when someone else is willing to make it for you?"

I don't wait for her to answer. I turn and plow up the stairs to my room, because tears are coming now, and I don't want to give her the satisfaction of seeing me cry. She'd think I was crying about my speech, or how much trouble I'm in, but my tears have nothing to do with that. At all.

## 33.

"Lines Written in Dejection on the Eve of Great Success"
—1959

I slam my bedroom door so hard my windows shudder, and I throw myself on the bed, still fighting back tears. Like a reflex, my eyes go straight to the collage above me, and I almost laugh at how ridiculous it seems now, with its sparkles, and quotes, and images of something that doesn't exist.

I get up. Balance on my mattress and rip it off the ceiling in one swift motion. I tear it in pieces, sending glitter and magazine clippings to the floor all around me. And then I sit down right where I'm standing, put my face in my hands, and cry. I cry over so many things—Julianna and Shane, and Orion and their sad, sad story. Kat and me, and the way things are already shifting and changing between us. Trevor, and that kiss that could have been so perfect.

I cry over how lost and powerless I feel, and how terrible I know my words have surely made my mom feel. But most of all I cry over how foolish I was to think I could actually change anything. Sitting here in my room, nothing has changed. I *almost* brought Julianna back to Orion, *almost* had a chance at something real with Trevor, was *almost* brave enough to tell my mom that her plan for me had stopped fitting. But almost moments don't count, and it all comes down to the choices I could've made but didn't.

And now I'm faced with a situation I don't have a choice in. I will have to go to that scholarship dinner tomorrow night, and I will have to stand up in front of all those people and give a speech I have yet to write. The irony of the fact that the pieced-together, Googled speech won my mom's approval is not lost on me. Of course she would applaud the stolen words of famous overachievers. It almost makes me want to deliver it just to make a point.

But I can't get up there and speak someone else's words, even if I don't have any of my own.

The ride to the restaurant where the reception will be held is silent, like the last day and a half have been. I haven't talked to Kat or heard from Trevor. Shortly after our fight my mom came into my room, took my phone and computer, and left without saying a thing. We've moved around each other since, with me only leaving my room when I could hear she was in hers, and her avoiding me completely. I've never gone this long without talking to another person, and she's never gone this long without speaking to me. It's clear, here in the car, that she doesn't plan on breaking the streak.

The *click clack* of the turn signal, the sound of the car accelerating then shifting as we drive up Main Street, all these things are exaggerated and loud in the silence between us. I fidget with my dress—a "smart" black one she picked out for me when we went to tour colleges. I'd hated it then just as much as I do now, but I didn't dare come downstairs in anything else.

A wave of sadness washes over me as we approach the corner where Kismet sits. It's evening now, and with the lights shining warm inside, it looks like a happy, inspired place. I don't see anyone behind the counter, but I picture Orion in the back room somewhere, burying himself in work, his path solitary without Julianna. And hers is the same. That's what seems the most sad to me—that neither of them even think there's a possibility they can be together.

We drive one more block and pull into the parking lot, get out, and walk up the stairs to the restaurant without speaking. A man in a black suit greets us and sends us to our table, where there are two older couples, presumably members of the scholarship board and their spouses, already seated. I look around the room at the few other tables. Each is a mix of kids I know from school, their parents, and the requisite board members, most of whom are already engaged in friendly-looking conversations with the other finalists. Nervousness rolls through my stomach hard, and I want to turn and walk out right then, but my mom clears her throat and gives me a nudge, and I put on my best smile and address the man seated closest to the place with my name on it.

"Hello," I say tentatively. "I'm Parker Frost, and this is my mother, Diana."

The elderly gentleman stands. "Pleased to meet you, Miss Frost." We shake hands. "I'm Sid McCoy, foundation president, and this is my wife, Betty." The woman seated next to him nods and smiles politely.

"Pleased to meet you both," I say. And then I have a silent panic attack. Of course I would be seated with the foundation president.

"Thank you so much for having us," my mom adds. "It truly is an honor."

Mr. McCoy nods. "Please, sit," he says with a warm smile. We do, and he settles back into his own seat too. Before I have a chance to worry about what to talk about, he says, "Frost. Like the poet. Do you know his work?"

"I do," I say, and I thank God that I do, and that he asked me about that instead of my having gone missing, like my mom was so sure everyone would. I'm so relieved I continue. "Actually, my father is a huge fan, and he passed that on to me early. 'Stopping by Woods on a Snowy Evening' was the first poem I learned by heart." I smile and keep my attention on Mr. McCoy. I don't have to look at my mom to know her smile has probably tightened at the mention of my dad, but I had to answer the man's question.

"Ah," he smiles. "One of my all-time favorites, after 'The Road Not Taken,' of course. One traveler, two roads, and an inevitable choice."

"One that he won't know was right or wrong until he's

lived with it," I say, and again I thank God for my dad and his love of Frost. I am much better prepared for a discussion on the ambiguities of this poem with the foundation president than I am to give a speech.

Mr. McCoy raises an eyebrow. "Precisely," he says. "Your father taught you well." My eyes jump to my mom at this, and I can see the hurt flash quick over her face. "It doesn't surprise me," he continues, "considering the depth of his own talent."

This *does* surprise me. "You know my father's work?"

Mr. McCoy nods. "I do. He has that same ability as the original Frost, to take a simple moment and transform it into something more with his words." He smiles. "I'm guessing that since you're here, you've probably got a bit of that magic yourself."

Before I can respond, a woman I don't recognize hurries over, all nervous excitement. She gives me a kindly glance, then turns to Mr. McCoy. "I am so sorry to interrupt, but it's time we get started."

My stomach drops, and Mr. McCoy nods and pushes his chair back, then looks at me. "I suppose we'll have to continue this discussion over dessert."

I nod weakly. My mom squeezes my knee under the table, and I put my hand over hers. An apology of sorts. Mr. McCoy strides to the podium at the front of the restaurant and taps the mic. Discussions hush, and forks still. I think I might be sick.

"Good evening," he says, "My name is Sid McCoy, and I would like to welcome you all to the annual Cruz-Farnetti

Scholarship dinner. This year marks a decade that we've come together to honor and remember Shane Cruz and Julianna Farnetti, two of our own, whose lights were extinguished before they had a chance to reach their full potential." He pauses and turns to their pictures behind him, and the audience nods in acknowledgment before he goes on. I look around at the other finalist tables, taking in the competition, wondering what they're going to say. There are four of them—all honors students, all earning inflated GPAs, all with potential to spare.

I swallow hard as Mr. McCoy continues. "We are not here tonight to dwell on that loss, but rather to celebrate the lives they led for the short time they were here. Lives that were lived to the fullest while they had the chance. We, the board of the Cruz Foundation, would like to give that same chance to a deserving individual here tonight by awarding a complete, four-year scholarship to the winner's chosen university."

I glance again at the other finalist's faces. Look for some indication that they're as panicked as I feel right now. Mr. McCoy continues.

"The process of choosing this individual is a rigorous one. In addition to reviewing the academic records of the nominees, we take into consideration teacher recommendations, extracurricular activities, and involvement in community service. All of those factors tell us about the strengths and talents of these individuals. But the reason we are gathered here tonight is more important than the sum total of all of those things. Tonight, we are here to listen to each candidate speak, and within their words, to learn more about the spirit of each of them. Every year we look for an individual who, like Shane Cruz and Julianna Farnetti, possesses something special. Something beyond what we can see on paper. I welcome you to listen to each of these students with that in mind. We will begin in alphabetical order by last name."

He pauses just long enough for me to realize that means I'm first, which is also long enough to wish I were anywhere but here at this moment.

"So, without further ado, I would like to introduce to you our first nominee, whom I had the pleasure of meeting already, Miss Parker Frost."

My heart leaps into my throat and I slide my chair back, taking the napkin from my lap. My mom puts a hand on my shoulder as I reach into my purse and pull out a black-and-white composition book. "You've got this, Parker," she says.

I nod, unconvinced, then on shaky legs weave my way through the tables of people who watch me expectantly. I'm supposed to be the shoo-in. I've worked to be the shoo-in. But with each step I take, I feel more unsure of myself. I hadn't expected to have to live up to my dad's words on top of everything else. The room is silent when I reach the podium, and the microphone picks up the rustling as I set my composition book in front of me. I look up with a smile I have to force, and sweep my eyes over the audience. It's now or never.

I clear my throat. Try for a smile. "Good evening. As Mr. McCoy said, I'm Parker Frost, and I'm honored to be here tonight. Um." I clear my throat again, and the volume of it over the mic is loud and awkward. I hear myself take another deep breath, and with this one, I decide. I will tell them what I know.

The first sentence comes out sounding timid. "Tonight I want to tell you about a teacher at our school, and a project he does every year." I glance at my mom and see the surprise and alarm I expect. This is not the speech she thought I was practicing up in my room.

I take a deep breath and continue, gaining a tiny measure of confidence. "Mr. Kinney is one of those rare teachers who truly inspires his students. Every year he gives his seniors two things: one of these"—I hold up the book—"and a question to answer. It comes from a poem by Mary Oliver, and it asks this: 'What is it you plan to do with your one wild and precious life?'" I let the line hang there a moment, hoping the audience understands just how important this question is before I go on.

"His students spend the last few weeks of their senior year writing their answers down in these before they seal them up and turn them in. And ten years later, when they've probably forgotten their answers to that question even exist, he sends them back to those same students.

"As Mr. Kinney's TA this year, I consider myself an honorary member of his class, so I wrote my speech in this book, and tonight I'm going to try and answer that question. It's a big one." I laugh nervously and get a few sympathy laughs in return.

I look down at my messy notes scrawled over the first page. The room is silent, all eyes on me. I recognize Mr. and

Mrs. Cruz sitting attentively at the front table, half-smiling, like I've already impressed them. I glance at my mom, who leans forward, chewing her lip and wringing her hands without any idea that's what she's doing. I try and remember to breathe.

"Up until recently, I had a plan for my one wild and precious life, and it's one I've stuck to for as long as I can remember. It's pretty simple, really. The plan has always been to study hard, get good grades, get into Stanford, study hard, get more good grades, and eventually become a doctor." I glance up at the audience again and see nods of approval all around. "I've got a lot of those boxes checked off already. This scholarship can definitely help with the rest.

"So I've stuck to this plan. I've spent plenty of nights studying instead of going out to parties. I've put in community service hours instead of taking spring break trips. I've gone the extra mile, put in the extra time, devoted everything I could to these things so that nothing could be left to chance, because chance, after all, can be dangerous.

"But what I didn't realize all that time, what I missed all along, is that chance is everywhere. It's also what life is made of. It's all around us, but most of the time we never see it working. We turn left instead of right, we take the stairs instead of the elevator, cross the street for no apparent reason. Our lives are made of these little moments that somehow add up, and sometimes, if we look back, we can see chance at work.

"When we turned left we found something we were looking for, when we took the stairs we avoided something not meant for us. When we crossed the street, we met the person who was. Looking back it's easy to see all those things. To connect the dots and see that it was actually those things that made all the difference." I glance at Mr. McCoy, who seems appreciative of the reference.

"But sometimes life gives us those rare moments where we *do* see chance as it's happening. And in those moments, we have a choice. And sometimes we have to take a risk. And it's scary. It makes us vulnerable. But I know now it's worth it.

"A few weeks ago I had one of those moments where I thought I saw chance at work, and a few days ago, I made a choice. I took a risk for something I totally believed in, and I failed. And right now, it still stings, but I'm glad I did it. I'm glad I did it, because I was about to leave high school without ever having taken a real chance on anything, or kissed the boy I've had a crush on since seventh grade, or stayed out past curfew and come home at sunrise. I was going to leave here without doing any of that. Because I was scared." I look at my mom now.

"Two days ago, I did a few of those things." I almost smile at the thought, but then the moment I pulled back from Trevor's kiss rushes back at me and I falter.

I look down at the page of notes in front of me. I had planned to go on about how doing those things made me realize how winning this scholarship would be another one of those important, life-changing things for me, and how I would take the opportunity and make the most of it, make them all proud. But I lose my place on the page.

I think of Julianna, and her refusal to take another chance on life and love, and Orion, who's lived his life avoiding the same kinds of vulnerability. And then I think of Kat, who's taken every chance that ever presented itself. And finally Trevor, who took so many on me, for so long. And then I realize.

I look around at this roomful of people, the Cruzes, who are still smiling at me like they want me to succeed, my mom, who is leaned forward in her chair now, probably having to restrain herself from getting up and finishing the speech for me. Mr. McCoy, who tries to encourage me with a nod. I can see them all willing me to finish. To give them a reason to believe that this scholarship is what I want most.

And in this moment, I know it's not.

"I'm so sorry," I say into the microphone, "but I don't think I'm the right person for this scholarship." A surprised murmur rolls through the audience, and Mr. McCoy gives me a quizzical look. My mom's jaw drops. "I used to be so sure—about my plan, and Stanford, and what I wanted out of life. All of it. But I'm not anymore. And I think this scholarship should go to someone who is." I swallow hard. "Thank you so very much for the opportunity, and for your time, but I would like to withdraw my name from your consideration."

I close the composition book. Back away from the mic. My mom stands up, horrified.

I turn and bolt.

## 34.

### "A Boundless Moment"
#### —1923

I burst out the restaurant doors into the night without any idea of where I'm going. The air is crisp, and burns my lungs and fogs around me as I run. My heart pounds with the realization that I just gave up my scholarship. I just walked—no, ran—away from a chance I was about to be handed. That I've been working toward for as long as I can remember. I stood at the podium, and I made that choice.

And now I don't know what comes next.

I can't know, until I've walked the road I've chosen. I slow at the thought. I don't have a plan, and there is no map for this. It's terrifying, but there's a spark of exhilaration that gives me hope that the choice I just made could turn out to be right, and this feels infinitely better than the weight of regret.

I hear a car behind me on the road, see it slow down as it passes, the driver none other than Debbie Monroe. She doesn't stop or offer me a ride, but she'll no doubt report to my mom the next time she sees her that I was walking the streets at night by myself in a dress not suited for the cold, and that maybe I should be better looked after. At the thought of my mom I feel bad. Not just about how shocked and panicked she must've been when I ran out, but about the things I said to her. I do regret those, and I know when I get home I'll have to face the choices I made about that.

Up until tonight, I thought that making big choices took courage—more than I had. But what I realize, here, now, is that it's not actually making the choice that takes courage. It's facing it afterward. Owning up to it, whether it's good or bad. I think of my mom and dad, and how even now they blame each other for the choices they made years ago. I think of Julianna and how she made a choice that she still hasn't forgiven herself for, and of Josh, who never got the chance to make the one that mattered most.

And then there's me.

I don't want to be like any of them. I stop walking and look up at the stars shining clear and bright in the moonless sky, and I promise them I never will be.

Another set of headlights approaches from behind, stretching out my shadow in front of me. The engine slows to a near idle, and I can tell this car is going to pull over. Of course my mom is out looking for me after that. Okay then. I stop, take a deep breath, and turn around, ready.

When I do, I see Kat's little red pickup. She pulls up right beside me and throws the passenger door open before I can reach for it. "Get in."

I do, slamming the door behind me.

She turns down her music and looks me over in the light from the dash. "You're insane. And you're gonna be in the deepest shit of your life for pulling what you just did."

"What? Were you—"

"The guys in the kitchen let me in the back so I could watch. I wasn't gonna miss your big moment." She shakes her head, almost laughing. "You looked scared shitless when you walked up there and stood behind that podium, but then once you started talking, you were like a whole different person. You shocked the hell out of everyone, P. God, I was proud of you."

She smiles, but it's gone in a second and worry creases her face. "But are you sure? I hope you didn't do that because of the things I said about you leaving. Maybe they'll still give it to you. Maybe they'll be so impressed by your balls that they'll—"

"I don't want it," I say. "And it's not because of anything you said. It's because of everything I said."

Kat looks unconvinced. "But what are you gonna do?"

"I don't know yet," I say, glancing out the window. "Maybe figure out what I *want* to do?"

We sit quiet for a long moment before Kat turns in her seat so she's facing me completely. "We should go to Kismet. There's something you need to hear." Her face is serious at first, but then a smile slides over it.

My stomach flutters. "What?"

"A love story," Kat says, and she puts the truck in gear.

We push through the door, jangling the bells, and warmth and the smell of espresso envelop us. Kat grins and I look around suspiciously. The place is empty, but nothing seems amiss.

Just then Lane walks out from the back room, bleary-eyed and hair wild, like he just rolled out of bed. "Hey, ladies," he croaks, sounding like it too.

Kat sidles up to the counter, still smiling, and leans on her elbows. "I need you to tell her what you told me."

Lane glances at me, seeming confused. "That you should come back after I close up?"

I burst out laughing. "I didn't know it was gonna be *that* kind of love story."

Kat rolls her eyes, trying to hide a smile. "*No,* about Josh."

Lane heaves a bag of coffee beans up on his shoulder and pours it into the grinder, then flips it on. "HE LEFT TOWN FOR A FEW DAYS," he yells above the noise.

"WHAT? WHERE?"

He switches it off, and Kat gives him a nod to continue. "Tell her."

"I don't know. But I think it must've been some kind of emergency, because he got a phone call this morning, went all white, and then hung up and offered me double my pay to watch the place until he gets back. Round the clock." He rubs his eyes. "Then he sat down at one of the tables and didn't say anything for a long time. I was pretty sure somebody died, but he seemed so messed up about it I didn't wanna ask."

"He didn't say where he was going?" A tiny hope flutters in my mind.

Lane shakes his head. "No. But then he did something kinda weird." Kat grabs my arm and squeezes at this.

"What?" I ask. "What did he do?"

"He took one of the paintings off the wall," Kat interrupts, no longer able to control herself.

I know before my eyes find the blank spot on the wall which one it is, and my heart pounds when I see that I'm right. "He took that painting with him? The one that was right there?"

"YES!" Kat yells.

Lane looks startled. Or slightly irritated. "Yeah, that one. Took it down and booked it outta here without looking back."

"Oh my God," I say, shaking my head. I almost don't believe it, but it couldn't be anything else. I laugh out loud and grab Kat's hands.

"Now why would he do a thing like that?" Kat asks, doing the thinking man's pose on the counter. "What do you think that could possibly mean?" The way she says it tells me she somehow knows what it could mean.

"I don't—"

"I think it means you're a shitty liar, P."

"Why?" I ask, still trying to wrap my head around what it could really mean.

Kat looks me in the eye. "I know you found her," she says. "I knew it was gonna be her as soon as I saw the paintings in that gallery. It was obvious the same person did them."

Now I'm lost. "Then why'd you pick a fight and leave?"

"So I could tell Josh."

Panic and my promise to Julianna zip through me on a wave of anger.

"I knew you wouldn't want me to," she says, looking apologetic. "Which is why I didn't go through with it. And then when you showed up all depressed, without the journal, and it was obvious it didn't go how you wanted, I was so frickin' thankful I didn't."

I release the breath I didn't know I'd been holding. "So you never told him? Anything?"

"No. It wasn't my place. It was your thing."

"Then . . ." My mind races ahead, connecting shiny, hopeful dots. "That phone call he got?"

Kat holds her hands out. "Had nothing to do with me."

"Oh my God," I whisper, picturing the moment Josh picked up the phone. "It had to be her." I look at Kat. "Right?"

"Had to be."

I can barely contain the soaring feeling within my chest. The thought of them together somewhere in the night makes everything seem right. Almost.

"I need a ride," I say suddenly.

A wide smile breaks over Kat's face, and she reaches into her purse for her keys. "I was wondering how long it would take you to say that." She loops her arm through mine. "I bet there's someone sitting at home right now, wondering the same thing."

There is one light on in Trevor Collins's house, and I hope with every last bit of me that it's his.

"You want me to wait here?" Kat asks.

I take a deep breath. "No. If this all goes terribly wrong I'll need the walk home anyway. If it goes right then, we'll see."

"That's my girl. Now go get your boy."

I open the door, step out into the crispness of the night, and try to breathe in courage. When I close it, Kat rolls down the window. "Carpe diem, P." I nod, she gives me a thumbs-up, and then she's gone. And I'm standing alone in my black dress, my hair messy from my impromptu run, about to ask the guy who's given me a million chances for one more.

At the door I hesitate. It's a reflex. A habit. One that comes from fear I don't want to have anymore, so I force myself to knock. My heart pounds, but the house is silent. Then I hear something. Footsteps. And then the door opens, and Trevor's right there looking surprised and confused, and I feel the same way, but I step into him before he can say anything.

I bring my lips to his fully, intentionally, their cold meeting his heat, in a kiss meant to tell him all the things I've been too afraid to say until right now. It takes him a second to catch up, but when he does his hands come to my face, then slide back into my hair, pulling me closer as he kisses me deeper, and all the times I've imagined this happening never came close to what I feel right now. I sink into it completely, letting everything else fall away so all that's left is this. A moment like a poem.

## 35.

"I shall be telling this with a sigh
Somewhere ages and ages hence.
Two roads diverged in a wood, and I,
I took the one less traveled by,
And that has made all the difference."
—*"THE ROAD NOT TAKEN,"* 1916

I can't know for sure that when Josh got the phone call that made him take the painting and leave, the person on the other end of the line was Julianna. There's no way to prove that she changed her mind and reached out, past her secrets, and beyond ten years to find him again. But I honestly can't see it any other way.

I sit on my roof, blanket wrapped around my shoulders, and watch as the first hint of light pales the edges of the sky and the stars begin to disappear. And just like I have every day since that night, I choose to believe that somewhere, under this same sky, they are together. That they will wake to the rising sun after a night spent entwined under the stars that led them back together. Like Romeo and Juliet at dawn. Except there will be no worry, or fear, or reason they shouldn't spend every morning for the rest of their lives this way. They've done nothing wrong, and they don't have to hide anymore. The threads of their stories are finally reconnected.

I watch the light from the rising sun spread out slowly behind the mountains. It's pale at first, but deepens to a rich gold in an instant, softening the sharp peaks and making the moment feel like a gift before it disappears into day. It's one of those moments I think Frost was talking about when he wrote "Nothing Gold Can Stay." I see it differently now. Not as a sad thing, but as a truth of nature. And life. Things have to change.

Since the night I made my choice and I'm certain Julianna made hers, everything has changed. Josh hasn't come back to Kismet. Kat's been helping Lane run it for the last two weeks, and showing a talent for managing I always knew she had. I haven't seen Trevor since the night I kissed him. He's off in Colorado, chasing the last bit of the season's snow for spring training, but we talk every day. And me. I've been here, forging a tentative understanding with my mom about what comes next. We both agree that whatever it is, there needs to be trust between us—enough to let go.

It was easy for her to think of letting go when it meant I was going to Stanford to chase after the goals she'd decided on for me. But letting me go so I can pack up and go spend some time with my dad is harder for her. He called the day after I walked out on the scholarship and said she'd told him everything. And that he was proud of me for all of it. And in the hours that we spent talking after that, laughing back and forth over memories, and musing about the future and writing and the genius of Robert Frost, we made a plan.

A breeze rolls soft over my cheeks and flutters the pages of the journal in my lap. My journal. Today I'll seal it up and bring it to Mr. Kinney, and tomorrow, after graduation, I'll get on a plane, and cross endless miles of land and sky, to begin the next chapter of my one wild and precious life. I don't know where I'll be ten years from now when my story comes back to me, but I hope that when I read it I can see that the road I chose really did make all the difference.

Mr. Kinney is taping up a cardboard box labeled SENIOR JOURNALS when I step into his classroom. "Is it too late for one more?" I ask.

He looks up and smiles. "Parker, hi. Of course not. Bring it here." I cross the rows of empty desks, and he pulls back the strip of tape he just put on. "I'm glad to see you decided to do one after all."

"Me too," I say, not sure what to add. I look down at the manila envelope in my hands one last time before I hand it over. "Thank you."

"It's no problem." He slips it in with the others and re-closes the flaps of the box before he grabs the tape. "So. I hear you deferred your acceptance."

I nod. "They call it a 'gap year.' A little extra time to gain some experience and save some money before going straight in to school. I'm going to be spending it with my dad in New York at the writing school where he teaches. Maybe take some classes there."

"That's great. Great news. You'll love it there." He rests his hands on the box and looks at me. "And I think it fits. You were a great writer even back in ninth grade, when I had you in my class."

I look at the ground, self-conscious about the smile this puts on my face. I'd worked hard at it. Especially because he was a fan of my dad's work. "Wow, thank you."

Kinney smiles. "I mean it, Parker. You're bright, and tal-ented, and you're going to shine at whatever you decide to do in life."

The way he says it is like a simple fact, and though I'm a little nervous about what lies ahead, I also believe him. "Thank you," I say again.

He stretches a piece of tape out over the top of the box and seals it up in one final motion. "All right. Into the vault with it. Or in my case, the closet." He hefts up the box and I open the closet door, and when I close it, it's with a finality that feels fitting.

Mr. Kinney sits down behind his desk. "Well, Parker Frost, can't wait to see where that journal finds you ten years from now."

"Me neither." I smile and turn to go, and that's when I see Mr. Kinney's quote for the day, a parting thought scrawled out in his messy writing over the whiteboard.

*"In three words I can sum up everything I've learned about life: It goes on."*

*—Robert Frost*

# ACKNOWLEDGMENTS

I am beyond grateful to so many people who were there for me during the writing of this book. First off, my family, for their endless support and belief in me, especially during those times I doubted myself. Second, I would like to thank my agent, Leigh Feldman, and her amazing assistant, Jean Garnett, for knowing when I needed support and when I needed to be pushed, and doing both of those things with grace and humor. Next, my editor, Alexandra Cooper, who has the vision to see the story that's in my mind, and the wisdom to somehow tease it out onto the page. There truly isn't a page in this book that hasn't benefitted from her insight and heart. I would also like to thank the entire Simon & Schuster family for their astounding talent and support—Justin Chanda, whose love for what he does is evident in *everything* he does; Lizzy Bromley, for her artistic talent and a cover more beautiful than I could have dreamed of; Amy Rosenbaum, for her hard work, contagious enthusiasm, and ability to sound like she's smiling in every e-mail she writes; Lydia Finn and Paul Crichton, for always being open to new ideas and for offering their constant support. I would also like to extend my deepest gratitude to Michelle Fadlalla and the superstar Simon & Schuster Education and Library team—Venessa Carson, Anthony Parisi, and Dawn Ryan, who are out there at every conference, putting the books into readers' hands, and spreading their excitement about them with heart, enthusiasm, and style. I could not be more honored to work with each and every one of these people. And I could not be more honored to count myself a member of the YA community, made up of so many readers, librarians, bloggers, and booksellers whose passion and support amazes and humbles me. Finally, I owe a special thank you to the writer friends I've made along the way, people I've come to depend on for the things that get me through—a shoulder to cry on, a kick in the pants, a streak of inspiration, a companion "in the weeds", or a shared laugh over a glass of wine. Carrie Harris, Elana Johnson, Gretchen McNeil, Stasia Kehoe, Lisa Schroeder, Sarah Ockler, Morgan Matson, Heidi Kling, and Corey Whaley, you are those people, and I hope that in time, I can return all that you've given me.